# The Dark Sea War Chronicles

## Volume I

# FIGHTING THE SILENT

### BRUNO MARTINS SOARES

ISBN: 9781549840098

*For Tiago, my nephew (a.k.a. Shorty).*

# CONTENTS

# ACKNOWLEDGMENTS

Thank you to all my friends and partners who helped me so
much, including:
Luís Madeira Rodrigues
Célia Cambraia
Nuno Madeira Rodrigues
Leonor Hungria
Cláudio Jordão
Rodrigo Martins Soares
Rodrigo Rahmati
Susana Almeida
And many others!

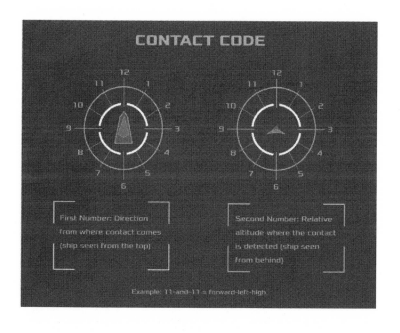

CONTACT CODE

First Number: Direction from where contact comes (ship seen from the top)

Second Number: Relative altitude where the contact is detected (ship seen from behind)

Example: 11-and-11 = forward-left-high.

# INTRODUCTION

*Kaptin* Worf Tinnzer scratched his itchy beard as he waited for his crewmen to complete their tasks on the bridge of S62.

Usually, no one shaved in the service. The Styllmarinne was an elite service unlike any other in the Riggsmarinne, the fierce Space-Navy of the republic of Axx. Silent Boats, or Styllebuutz, were out in deep space for much longer stretches than average ships, supplied out there by special vessels, pirate traders, occasional merchants and lonely outposts. They were isolated for a long time. So the men didn't shave. At one point, the *Addmiralis* had tried to introduce shaving machines in the service, but no one actually used them. It had become an honor thing, a badge of the bravest, the famous beard of the *Styllemarinners*. They wouldn't wash either, so after a day or two, there would be this characteristic omnipresent stink. So omnipresent, in fact, that they would fail to notice it at all.

He thought of his wife, Sondra, and of his young son, Worf. He hoped they would be okay. They were far from any important target down there, in the castle, the thousand-year-old family home in the middle of the woods.

As safe as they could be.

Worf looked through the visor from his seat in the center of the bridge. Silent Boats didn't have scanners all around because they messed up the refracting camouflage. They had typically three probe levels with very small probes circling around the vessel. The captain's visor was a bulky face-covering helmet Worf had to slide down pushing a button on the arm of his chair. As his left fingers managed more buttons, the chair was made to rotate, giving him the view of Space around the Silent.

"*Kapt,* a message from S60, she's here as well."

"All right."

That was the third boat. They were ready. It was time. Worf looked at the enemy. More than 40 vessels. A loaded convoy.

"Has 63 set the time?"

The instructions were that the first boat on the scene would take point and coordinate the attack.

"Just a minute, *Kapt.*"

"Ask them about the position as well."

"Yes, *Kapt.*"

"As it is, might as well follow them all the way to Webbur." Said Rukt, the Navigator.

S62 had been in position for over 20 hours, now. If this were a normal operation, the attack would have occurred many hours ago. Worf knew the men were starting to get impatient. He pushed the button, and the helmet went up, freeing his head.

"Might as well service our ship in the Brury moon also." Continued the Nav.

People laughed. Worf's calm, cold voice, crossed the bridge:

"That's enough, Rukt."

They all settled down. They waited. Finally, the Comms Officer looked at the Captain.

"Time set to 30 minutes, *Kapt.*"

"Alright. They gave us position?"

"Position B. Starboard side."

"Alright."

*Lüivettenand* Urster smiled as he approached with a tea cup in his hand.

"It seems they're going to chain us up out here as well. *Ver-Kaptin*. I'd rather we were free as before." He whispered.

Worf sipped the tea. Urster had spiked it, as usual.

"We're at war. We have to be effective."

"What would they know about that?"

Worf was displeased with the comment. He lowered his voice so only Urster would hear him.

"Careful, Urster. This is no place for politics."

"My point exactly."

Worf clinched his teeth.

"Enough. I'll put you in the brig myself. This is not politics, it's good tactics."

Since Urster's brother had disappeared in the Tribunal's Seichr prison, the officer's remarks had become more and more bothersome. Every time he opened his mouth, Worf feared for him. Even on a small ship like this where the crew was tighter than family, there were people loyal to the regime. They could all get in trouble, if Urster didn't stop his dangerous comments.

For now, Urster backed off. The Engineer, Karolu, entered the bridge. Worf knew something was wrong. What would he be doing here as they were minutes away from action?

"*Ver-Kaptin*."

"What is it, Karolu?"

"I'm sorry to bother you at this hour, but I need to warn you."

Worf sighed.

"The reactor?"

"Yes, *Kapt*. It's fine now. But if we need to fight..."

"How much time would it run if it cracks?"

"One hour, one day, one week. Not sure, *Kapt.*"

Worf thought for a moment, then shrugged his shoulders.

"Nothing we can do now. We're committed. Just take care of it the best you can. If all goes as usual, we won't have to fight."

"Nothing usual with this operation, *Ver-Kaptin.*" Said Urster.

Worf looked at his second, raising his eyebrow.

"We're committed." He repeated.

"I'm just saying. Anything could happen."

"We're committed." Said Worf once more. They all paused. Finally, both Urster and Karolu backed down.

"Yes, *Kapt.*"

"Yes, *Kapt.*"

Worf finished his tea in silence, while the whole crew prepared for the attack. There was nothing more he needed to do. They all knew very well the business of the day. Finally, Urster looked at him.

"We're ready, *Kapt.* 'T' minus 5 minutes."

Worf looked up, nodded, sat back on his chair and pushed the button, so the helmet descended on his head. In seconds, he was looking outside. Black all around. Through the zoom and the enhancement protocol, he could pick up the ships on his bow.

"All right." He said, with his head inside the helmet. "Do we have the targets' ID confirmed?"

"Yes, *Kapt.* Merchant ship *Solio,* 800k, and merchant ship *Harvy,* 700, are the first."

"Escort?"

"The nearest threat is the *Nyban,* a Corvette. Old class. Not much firepower."

"All right." Worf's helmet showed him the enemy vessels. "Let's not push our luck with the reactor. We get the first two merchants, and we leave."

"Yes, *Kapt.*"

"Time, sir."

"All right. Increase to covert attack speed. Torpedoes?"

"Ready, *Kapt.*"

"63 is engaging, *Kapt.* Position A."

"All right. Rukt, we're deviating. Get us on target."

"Yes, *Kapt.* Sorry, *Kapt.*"

Worf rotated his chair to look at where S63 should be at that point. He had no visual on the other ship, but the friendly ID signal was pulsing a blue dot inside his helmet, so he knew where the other ship was. And also... In a strange move, an enemy ship was getting in an awkward position. It was decreasing speed and falling behind.

'What is that frigate doing?' Thought Worf.

BRUNO MARTINS SOARES

# EPISODE 1 - FIRST SHOT

"Look at that! *What a sight!*" Lara was looking down through the glass towards the surface of Webbur and the rotating spaceport. What a sight! I thought, but I was looking the other way. The fleet was already quietly assembling in formation, getting ready for the voyage. It was beautiful. It was in a 'spine formation.' A beautiful slick formation. (Little did I know it would soon become obsolete.)

I looked at Lara. She was still sighing at the planet. Her lovely *petite* ear sliding out from beneath the smooth blond hair with a little help from a finger. I smiled to myself and looked back at the fleet. The courier-corvette was climbing at a steady acceleration rate towards the big ships. The 2nd Fleet of the Webbur Union. One of the strongest in the system. The 1st Fleet, the First Admiral's fleet, also known as the Home Fleet, stayed close to the planet. The 3rd Fleet, the Outer Fleet, patrolled the vast desert frontier to put in check the menacing fleets of the Cold Empire. And the 2nd Fleet, my fleet, the Inner Fleet, controlled everything from here to the sun. No one else had such imposing ships. Not even the Kingdom of Torrance, with its magnificent legacy, and certainly not the Republic of Axx, for all its might. (Little did I know that would also change.)

And there she was. At the fleet's center, my ship. Admiral Hedde's ship, the *W.S.Magnar*, a 120-battery 1st class Battleship. You could hardly take your eyes off her when she was like this, her flank to the sun, surrounded by her subjects.

"I was talking about Webbur." Lara was looking at me, a smart smile across her face. I jumped inside. Not because she caught me looking the wrong way, but because she smiled at me and, for some reason, it always made me jump inside, surprised.

"Y-Yes, I know."

She smiled and, through the window behind her, I caught a glimpse of two more of the Fleet's Colossus: the *W.S.Taurus*, a 90-battery 2nd class Battleship; and behind her, the *W.S.Viker*, a 70-battery 3rd class.

"Is it true they give astonishing balls at the *Magnar?*" she said.

I blushed.

"Sometimes."

I looked out the window once more. Around the big ships, three destroyers were getting into a flank-protection position, and a fourth was on point, ahead of the *Magnar*. Two small 32-battery frigates traveled ahead and *Syrius,* the small but fast courier-corvette, was transporting us in. The 10 billion-ton bulge supply ship *W.S.Warhog*, and the smaller repair ship *W.S.Pleeto* completed the fleet, traveling behind and below the *Taurus*. 12 beautiful green-red-and-gray ships that spread wonder and might across the whole system.

"When's the next one?"

I was having a hard time thinking. Lara and I had been getting closer and closer these last few days, and the thought of leaving her at her post on the *W.S. Orink,* a 4th class 50-battery destroyer, flanking the *Magnar*, and not be with her for weeks, kept me in a constant state of shock. We had written many messages to each other, said many things online. But only in the last few days had we really been together, physically and mostly alone. And it still made me nervous. And it also made me excited and air-headed. And that had to stop really quickly because a Webbur warship is not a place to be nervous or air-headed. Or excited, for that matter. The problem was: I didn't want it to stop.

"Well," I said uncomfortably (I was still uncomfortable). "I suppose when we arrive in Torrance, an allied planet, with all fanfare, the Admiral will want to give a ball. I suppose…"

"Would a cute little nurse like me get invited?"

"If she was asked by a steady flag-ship junior officer like me, she would."

"Well…"

(Oh! Her smile… Her smile…)

"Should I be preparing for it, then?" She tilted her head, provokingly. (Oh! She tilted her head…)

"I guess you should…"

"Mr.Iddo, this is you, I believe" interrupted the master-of-the-corvette, warning me to get ready to leave and board the approaching *Magnar.*

I looked at Lara. She looked at me. It was a look of small desperation. She smiled. Joy and sadness in a smile. We looked around, trying to spot any on-looking eyes, and then we managed a fast, faint and intense kiss.

\*

15,000 people lived and worked on the *Magnar.* It was an impressive beast. It was made out of 12 different huge compartments, called hulls, with six ports and six starboards. Each hull was basically independent and could be isolated from the rest. It had its own hospital, cafeteria, sleeping quarters, gym, working areas, warehouse, armory, and gravity controls. Each hull harbored about 1,000 crew members. If attacked or depressurized, a hull would be blocked, cut off from the rest of the ship. It was calculated that the *Magnar* could lose 5 or 6 hulls before the ship became inoperable. The hulls were numbered: odds for port and even for starboard. So 1st Hull was at the bow on the left, and 2nd Hull was at the bow on the right, and 3rd Hull was on the left behind the 1st Hull and so on.

Besides the functions the hulls divided between themselves, like launching spacecrafts, managing the engines or conducting research, each hull was also responsible for 10 ten-tube High-Caliber High-Explosive missile batteries. The tubes could be fired in rapid succession so at any one time the *Magnar* could have on course the massive number of 1200 HCHE missiles. Together with the *Taurus* and the *Viker,* the big warships of the fleet could fire more than 3 thousand warheads at one time. Not counting destroyers and frigates. This was mighty power indeed.

The Main Bridge tower was a different ship segment than the main hulls. It lived for the Bridge. Even though every hull had its own commander, its own master and its own way of living, the Tower (as it was known) harbored almost a thousand people simply concerned with managing the whole ship, the whole fleet, and answering to the Admiral himself. It hosted more commanders, senior officers and junior officers than the whole of the ship combined, besides the Admiral, the Captain, and the First Officer. The commanders and officers of the main Commands and the C-Team, all lived there. Just above the living quarters were 5 Command HQ's, each made of a common working area and an office for the Commanding Officer. And the C-Team HQ, which had three offices: for the Admiral, the Captain, and the First Officer. Above the HQ's, was the Bridge. And above that, with a breathtaking view and already out of the protection of the armored main hull, was the Admiral's dining room, rarely used except for impressing special visitors. Then, the Captain's observation deck, for looking with naked eye at the ship and fleet, on the rare occasions it was needed. And finally, upstairs were the main upper deck sensors and antennas, with the occasional T-guy poking around.

*

I put my bag in my locker next to my bunk and looked in the mirror. I wouldn't stay in the cabin long, I'd rather present myself for duty as soon as possible, and one does not present oneself to senior officers in a slack uniform.

"Hey, Byl! Glad you're back."

I smiled, turned around and grabbed Ploom's hand. I shared the cabin with three other junior officers, and Ploom and I were the oldest ones in the flagship.

"Hi, Ploom. What do you say? Tight ship?"

"Yep, seems tight so far."

"Juniors?"

"Tight. No sissies or assholes."

"What does the master say?"

"Not much, so far."

"That's good. Who's this?"

Behind Ploom's large smile came a dark-faced shy boy, the youngest possible, trying to get into the pea-like cabin.

"This is Gaddy. He's with the T's."

Technical-Command, or T-Comm, was one of the five commands that made up the Captain's team on the bridge. The other four were Navigation, Signals, Logistics, and Weapons. Ploom was with the N's, and I was with the S's. We both belonged to the C-team, and that's why we had accommodations in the Main Bridge tower, just below the center of command, ready to get to our posts at a moment's notice.

"Nice to meet you, Mr.Gaddy."

"Please, call me Tym."

"A T's Tym," joked Ploom.

The fourth bunk in the cabin belonged to Hekk. He was a Marine lieutenant, a W., the Marine liaison on the bridge. If I knew him at all, he would be at the gym right now. In a few hours, I might be able to join him for some martial arts training.

"So," said Ploom, closing the door of the cabin. "Are we going to war?"

I sighed while I closed the top button on my uniform.

"Why would we be going to war, Ploom?"

"Oh, don't give me that, Byl. Axx is a hair away from getting up Torrance's ass. And Torrance is our ally. If they go to war, we won't be far behind. Isn't that the reason we're going on this trip? Letting the blue-eyes' know the *torries* won't stand alone?"

"If you say so, Ploom."

His face had a red surge of irritation. Of course, he was right. And I was in a better position to know because I belonged to S-Comm. All intelligence came through me. And I could tell him because he was C-team. He would be on the Admiral's bridge and had clearance. But Gaddy didn't. He worked at the T-Comm HQ, down in the belly of the beast, not up in the upper tower. And if Ploom was enough of an idiot not to care about it, I wasn't. So I stood ground and faced his stare until he backed down.

"Mr.Gaddy!" a strong voice came from the corridor. It was Sandars, the master-of-the-tower. His head popped inside. Gaddy turned his head.

"Hmmm? Sir?"

"Don't «Hmm-sir» me! You're not a God damn cow!"

"Yes, sir!"

"And don't call me «sir»! I work for a living!"

"Yes, Master Sandars!"

"You're a Tech-boy, aren't you, Mr.Gaddy?! I'd think

you lads would have the sense to check your SCD's once in a while!"

Embarrassed, Gaddy turned on his Ship-Communication-Device, forgotten on his collar.

"They're calling you down below on 2nd Hull, if you please! On the double!" roared Sandars. Gaddy stormed away. The master looked at me and nodded. "Glad to see you on board, Mr.Iddo."

"Glad to be here, Mr.Sandars."

As they left, I turned to Ploom.

"Don't go around talking about war like that, Ploom! It's a hot topic, and not everybody has clearance. We need to be careful."

Ploom smiled.

"Oh, never mind that. Just tell me about Lara!"

*

Most of the ship's inner corridors were well lit but narrow. Yet in a day like Launch-Day, even the wide main grid corridors were difficult to walk in, and everyone bumped into everyone. And just as the rest of the ship, the Tower was full of chaos and confusion on the corridors and escalators. There is a regular joke among space-sailors: «It's not by chance it's called L-Day.» This is because about 60 to 70% of all the confusion going on in the last few days before a launch is caused by Logistics crew members running around all stressed up. At any other time, they would be as active as anyone else. But just before L-Day all the pressure is on them, making sure everything is on board and in the right place. As I made my way up to S-Comm HQ, I kept dodging L-guys left and right, and I swear that up to this day I don't know how these guys don't get hurt more often with the speed they run all over the place on L-Day.

I finally got to Signal-Command HQ and found out

Commander Zell, the C.O., was not in.

"Admiral's quarters," they told me.

Good. That would give me time to look at the last signals coming in and get some work done.

\*

Zell leaned back from his desk and finally looked at me in his quiet manner. This was the first time I was his first lieutenant. The previous one had been promoted to a senior post in a warship of the 3rd.

"Had a nice leave, Mr.Iddo?"

"Yes, sir. Thank you, sir."

"Had a chance to look at the signals?"

"Yes, sir. Nothing major, sir."

"I need you to update the buoys' codes."

"Done that, sir."

"Then you need to figure out the compensation for the software upgrade and check in with Navigation."

"Done that as well, sir."

Zell raised an eyebrow. I smiled inside. It wasn't easy to impress him, and it felt really good.

"And...?" asked the C.O.

"I'm sorry, sir?"

"What did you get? What was the compensation?"

"Minus 1, sir."

Zell raised the other eyebrow and looked at his tablet on the desk.

"That's it?"

"Yes, sir."

"Minus 1?"

"Yes, sir."

He twisted his mouth, satisfied.

"That's not bad."

"No, sir."

He kept looking at his tablet, checking the numbers.

14

"They verified the calculations?"

"Not yet, sir."

"Tell me the minute they do."

"Yes, sir."

He leaned back again and looked straight at me, once more.

"Nice leave, then?"

"Yes, sir."

"Good. Don't expect another one for a while. Not until we get to Torrance, anyway."

"I won't, sir."

"The fleet will launch at 1800 hours. You're dismissed, Mr.Iddo."

"Sir!"

\*

"*Viker* is clear to launch, sir," I announced. "That's the last one."

"Very well, Mr.Iddo," responded Zell, then turning to the Admiral. "All clear to launch, sir."

The Main Bridge is a very special place. It usually accommodates around 18 crewmembers. It has 5 Weapons stations, 3 Navigation, 3 Signals, and 3 Technical. And also the L-commander (we called him the quartermaster, or the Q.) or his substitute. Then there are three high chairs, each one behind and above the other: the First Officer's chair, the Captain's chair, and the Admiral's chair. Officially, the ship was commanded by the Captain, leaving the Admiral to command the fleet. But nobody had any doubt it was Admiral Hedde who actually headed the *Magnar*. Hedde had risen through the ranks and never really gotten over the pleasure of leading a battleship. And Captain Simmas was happy to abide, as he deeply admired and trusted the Admiral.

"Ok," said the Admiral, a small solid looking man with

impeccable white hair and red and gray uniform. "Tell them to launch, Mr.Zell."

"Signal to launch, Mr.Iddo."

"Yes, sir! Launch, launch, launch!" I gave the orders to the other ships of the fleet, while I heard the Admiral calmly order:

"You can launch, Captain."

"Sir." Nodded Simmas, and then to Navigation: "Half speed ahead, Mr.Tumm."

"Yes, sir," said the N-Commander "Half speed ahead, Mr.Ploom."

"Yes, sir." said Ploom.

And the engines started to roar,the whole ship trembled, and we started to move.

What makes the Main Bridge of a warship a really special place to anyone who knows it is the surroundings. Even though we're in a solid wall armored sphere inside the ship, the walls all around us mimic the surroundings picked up by the sensors of the ship so, in fact, the bridge's stations' platform seems to be suspended in space, with nothing holding us. If you look up, down, left, right, forward or backward, you will see the space around the ship, the stars, the planets and the other ships. And the rotating stations are used to do just that: look everywhere. To someone not used to it, it gives you nausea, disorientation, and chills. But after a while, it grows on you, and it fascinates you. Especially when the whole fleet is starting to launch next to your home planet, and the movement becomes apparent. It's a fine spectacle. We called it a mimic display, or MID, for short.

I looked up and to my left, to a 3D hologram of the whole fleet suspended above my head. It was called the FCD, the Fleet Constellation Display, or simply the Constellation. It showed at each point the relative position of each ship in the fleet. I looked at the image of the *Orink* and imagined Lara looking at Webbur from a destroyer's watch as it flew by in lovely colors. I looked back at the starboard and believed for a moment I could see a glimpse of the real destroyer, guarding *Taurus*' flank.

After a few minutes, the Admiral got up, straightened his uniform and left, saying:

"The ship is yours, Captain."

"Sir!"

The Captain waited a bit more, then exchanged some words with the First Officer and finally said:

"You have the ship, Mr.Orrey."

"Sir!" And the Captain left, and Mr.Orrey turned to the rest of the bridge. "Officers are free to resume shift schedule."

And all the senior officers responded: "Yes, sir!"

And Zell turned to me and Dalto, the other Signals' junior officer on duty on the bridge (a new man, focused face, brown curls), and said:

"I'll be retiring now. Mr.Iddo, you wait until we clear the last moon and then you can go. Mr.Dalto will do first shift. Mr.Orta will relieve him afterward. You all have the shift schedule in your duty folders already. Mr.Dalto, anything you need, first talk to Mr.Iddo and then me. Understood?"

"Yes,sir!"

"Carry on, then."

*

Things started to go awry 6 days after L-Day. I was doing the graveyard shift on the bridge. Tumm, the N-Comm, a baldy and experienced officer everyone respected, was in the First Officer's chair, handling the bridge. And there were only 4 more people around: 2 in Navigation, 1 in Weapons and 1 in Technical.

For many, space traveling can be boring. It's always the same view, mainly black, with a starlight fabric on the immense horizon. Nothing really changes for many days in a row. But I liked it. It's peaceful. Quiet. Gives you time for yourself, your thoughts, and to breathe. The quiet hours on duty on the bridge, for me, were always a treat.

We were heading towards the Dark Sea. That's the vast empty space between the Mirox asteroid belt and the Eeron asteroid belt, towards the sun and the inner solar system, where Torrance and Axx faced each other. The Dark Sea was a dangerous place for many, where only pirates and bold merchants and armed supply convoys ventured, away from the influences of the armed forces of the different planets. It was also the 2nd Fleet's Area of Operations, where we were sent most of the time, to catch some overachieving pirate or assert Webbur's influence in the region.

I was minding my own business, looking at the empty, maybe thinking of Lara, when an orange sign popped up on my console. It was a warning from a Level 8 probe. I straighten up on my chair.

"Contact, sir. Level 8, 10-and-10, sir." (Meaning forward-left-high.)

Tumm looked at me.

"What kind of contact, Mr.Iddo?"

"I don't know, sir. I can't see it. But it's popping up on my screen. Two probes. Level 8."

"But you can't see it?"

"No, sir."

Rumens was on point at Navigation, so Tumm turned to him.

"Where are we, Mr.Rumens? Is it a rock already?"

"No, sir. We're still a day away from the Mirox."

We were all quiet for a few minutes. Nothing happened. Tumm turned to me again.

"How much time until you have to send another batch out, Mr.Iddo?"

"78 minutes, sir."

The *Magnar* and the fleet surrounded themselves with 12

levels of probes. Level 1 was the nearest one, the last-resort level, where the most immediate threats would be detected before reaching the sensor level of the ships themselves, 0-Level. And then there were 11 consecutive levels of probes, until the 12th, the farthest from the fleet. Probes were Signals' responsibility, along with communications. As they all had limited fuel and speed, they would be left behind after a while, and we needed to periodically send out another batch of football-size probes.

My console was silent. I could sense that Tumm was intrigued and uncomfortable. Two contact warnings from two different probes at Level 8 could hardly be a mistake, even though the probes seemed unable to show us anything. But Level 8 meant whatever it was had passed undetected through three levels of detection. One would be normal, two acceptable, but three? Maybe it was one of those strange natural phenomena space sailors are always rumoring about.

Then, another flag popped up on my screen.

"Contact, sir! Level 6, 10-and-10! No image!"

No one said anything, but I could hear Tumm touching his buttons, no doubt calling for higher rank officers on the bridge. After just a few minutes, several people started coming in. Young officers started to man their stations. Zell came in as well. He didn't speak. He just sat down beside me and looked at the screens. Finally, First Officer Orrey came in and sat on the Captain's chair, looking at his screens.

"Where are we, Mr.Tumm? Is it a stray rock?"

"Still a day away from the Mirox, sir."

"Very well. The ship is mine. Resume your duties."

"Sir! First Officer has the bridge."

Tumm left the First Officer's chair and went back to his N-Comm station. Orrey was in command. Everyone on this bridge was a well-respected and hand-picked experienced officer, but Orrey was a special one.

Commander Zell had once told me he would be a brilliant admiral, one day.

"Mr.Zell, would you please get word from the Kark and the Lion to what they are seeing?"

*Kark* and *Lion* were the two destroyers on the fleet's larboard flank. As I was on 'probe duty,' Zell contacted the ships himself.

"They confirm contacts, sir. No images."

Then the Captain got in and said.

"I have the bridge."

Orrey immediately got up and sat on his own chair, saying:

"The Captain has the bridge."

Simmas sat on Captain's chair, and everyone was silent while he got up to speed reading his screen.

"Red flag!" I almost shouted. "Level 5, 10-and-10! No image, sir!"

'Red Flag' meant a linear movement through three levels of probes, signaling there was a definite movement towards the fleet's ships. And there was still no image showing up on the screen. I had an irrational burst of shame for the probes not being able to see the contact, but it was easily overcome by a slight burst of fear and excitement.

"The *Kark* is clearing the boards, Captain." Said Zell.

"Ok," responded the Captain. "Clear the boards."

'Clearing the boards' was a first alert procedure. It meant all non-essential activities going on or planned for the next few minutes would be postponed or canceled. Nothing should be on the Boards of Activities but what the bridge would order. Everyone on the bridge got suddenly very busy calling everyone else on their Commands.

Orta, a brown hair nice guy who was my colleague in S-Command, finally got here and took his place. I glanced at Zell's screen and saw the signal: «To the fleet: *Magnar* is clearing the boards.»

We waited. Then I heard a calm voice coming from

behind and above me.

"Mr.Iddo, put the flags on the MID, if you don't mind."

I looked and saw Admiral Hedde looking at me.

"Sir!"

I sent the four warnings from the probes into the mimic display, for all to see. The little flags seemed to appear in the middle of the void, out there in the dark. They had all turned red, of course, showing the linear movement.

"So the last was 8 minutes ago?" asked the Admiral.

"Yes, sir."

"I see. So we don't know where it is, could be anywhere. Captain, get the alert up a notch, will you?"

"Yes, sir. Battle stations, Mr.Vallard," ordered the Captain to W-Command. "Mr.Zell, send the signal."

"Yes, sir. Mr.Orta, battle stations everyone."

"Sir!"

Orta began sending signals to everyone in the ship, while Zell sent the signals to the fleet. «To the fleet: *Magnar* called battle stations.» And then the Admiral spoke again.

"Mr.Vallard, get all odds ready, if you please."

"Yes, sir! All odds ready!"

'Odds' meant all port-side HCHE and projectile-defense missile batteries. From 1st Hull to 11th Hull, on the left, the W's would be 'cocking' their guns.

"Odds ready, sir!" announced Weapons.

"Thank you," said simply the Admiral.

And then Zell:

"All vessels called battle stations, sir."

"Very well."

Everyone was focused on their consoles. For a few minutes, nothing happened.

"Anything, Mr.Iddo?" asked Mr. Zell, at half voice.

"Negative, sir."

We kept waiting. Several minutes went by. The Admiral asked:

"How far are we to the Mirox, Mr.Tumm?"

21

"A day, sir."

"Hmm… Too far…"

We waited a bit more. The Admiral gave another order.

"Get the *Syrius* to circle port, please, Mr. Zell."

"Sir!"

Zell sent the signal, and the fast courier-corvette went on patrol on the larboard side of the fleet. After several minutes, Zell spoke again.

"*Syrius* is signaling no-contact, sir."

"Very well. "

The quiet wait went on for almost an hour. I kept looking at my console, but no new lights showed up. Nothing. And then the Admiral said:

"Ok. Signal to free the boards, Mr.Zell."

"Sir!"

And a signal was sent to resume all activities.

"Whatever it was, it's not there now." Added the Admiral, getting up. "Mr.Orrey, please get everyone downstairs. We need to talk about this. "

"Sir!"

\*

I was invited to go as well. There was always a junior officer from Signals in a special C-Team meeting so that external communications could be monitored from within the room. Now that I was second to Commander Zell, I was the one in. The Admiral headed the C-Team HQ conference table, and the Captain and First Officer were there, as well as all main Commanders (with the exception of Commander Mahar, from Technical, who had the bridge at this time). I was in a corner, manning the Signals' station.

"Well," started the Admiral. "What just happened?"

Everyone stayed quiet for a moment until Mr.Orrey said what most of us were thinking.

"I would say a Silent, sir."

'Silent Boats.' That's what we called the sneaky invisible little ships pioneered and developed to perfection by the Axx Republic. Many had them. There was even the rumor of one or two falling into the hands of pirates. But only Axx had them in number and relied on them the most.

Commander Torney, the Quartermaster, a skinny man with a razor sharp nose, made a nauseated face.

"That's impossible. No Silent can be out here in the middle of nowhere, stalking us. Not on this side of the Mirox, anyway. It wouldn't have the range."

Orrey twisted his mouth.

"That we know of…"

Captain Simmas cleared his throat.

"Mr. Zell, could it be a pirate ship? Supplied somewhere within the Mirox belt?"

Zell shook his head.

"The last reports tell us of no pirate activities from here to the Raven dwarf planet, sir. The Dark Sea buccaneers have been especially quiet, we're not sure why. "

Orrey spoke again:

"Of course, they would be especially quiet if there was unusual military activity in the region."

"What kind of unusual military activity? Whose?" asked the Q, frowning.

"I think we all know what Mr.Orrey is talking about," intervened the Admiral. "If it was a Silent, she had to be from Axx."

"But that's impossible, sir." Returned the Q. "We're too far."

"They've found a way," continued the Admiral. "Does anyone have any other possible explanation for what happened?"

No one said a thing. The Admiral nodded.

"I can't imagine any reason for a pirate ship to threaten a Webbur fleet like this, can you?"

"Defiance?" suggested Tumm. "For some of these lads,

it's a way of living."

"They would defy us by attacking a convoy and looting tourist ships. Not coming into this side of the Mirox and menacing the 2nd Fleet." The Admiral waved his hand. "No. It was a Silent, for sure. And it was a military one. And that means someone is flexing its muscles. And I would say it's Axx."

The room went quiet again. And at that precise moment, as if on cue, I got a signal on my screen. A priority signal. And I froze. I read it once and again. And finally, I got up, approached the table and said to Commander Zell's ear.

"Priority signal, sir."

The Admiral called:

"What is it, Mr.Iddo?"

I straightened myself up and looked at him, timid.

"Priority signal, sir."

"Yes?"

I hesitated.

"Spit it out, man!" shouted the Q.

"It's war, sir," I said. "Torrance declared war on Axx."

They all looked at each other, startled. Admiral Hedde leaned back.

"Well…" he said. "There it is."

\*

"Are we at war?"

Lara's beautiful face showed her fear and worry on the screen. The war had been announced to the fleet a few hours ago. But only now had I been able to call her.

"No, not yet," I answered as calmly as I managed. "Torrance is our friend and ally, but neither the President nor the Council have made that decision."

"But they will, won't they?"

"I don't know, Lara. I don't know. For now, I think

we're spectators."

"But are we still going to Torrance?"

"I don't know. The Admiral is maintaining course... I think he's waiting for orders."

She gave me a sad little smile and was as beautiful as ever. I wished I could just raise my hand and caress her soft skin, remove the stray hair from her forehead, raise her chin and kiss her pink almost-trembling lips. Her voice sighed through the channel.

"So there's not going to be a ball, is there?"

'A ball'... What a lovely girl... It was not the enemy she worried about.

"I don't think so, Lara."

She lowered her eyes, with true sadness.

"Oooh..."

\*

"So? Where's the buoy?"

The Admiral's voice echoed through the bridge. Zell looked at me, uncomfortable. Everyone looked at me.

"Do you have it, Mr.Iddo?" asked Zell.

"Negative, sir. Silence all around."

You might think from books or fictional recordings that an asteroid belt is a compact agglomerate of rock dangerously bumping against each other and getting you in trouble. In reality, it's more like a sea with a light population of icebergs, where you spot one or two rocks once in a while. However, it forced passing ships to change course several times and, at first, many would get lost as navigation became difficult and many of the minerals in the rocks themselves would interfere with some sensors. Using the sun for reference didn't always work, and many times travelers would come out of the asteroid belt in a very different spot than what they originally estimated, facing the sun but far from course. If fuel had been carefully rationed for a specific trip, it could turn a regular travel into a nightmare. And so, Webbur had set a string of navigation buoys on the Mirox asteroid belt, as did Torrance on the Eeron. Following those buoys' signals, any traveler could maintain course within the belt and come out where they should on the other side, along the path from Webbur to Torrance and back. Equipped with sophisticated pulsar navigation, the 2nd Fleet hardly needed the buoys, but still, it was procedure to use them whenever the course made it convenient. Yet, the first buoy seemed to be missing.

"Are the calculations correct, Mr.Zell?" asked the Captain. Everyone was on the bridge for the entrance into the Mirox. "Do we have the correct contact codes?"

"Yes, sir." Stated my C.O. without a doubt in his voice. "All calculations were rechecked and verified by Navigation. The buoy should be here."

The bridge was silent for a few moments. Finally, the Admiral spoke:

"Then can we find the next one, please?"

"Set your course, Mr.Tumm," said the Captain.

"Sir!"

I felt relieved by Zell's statement. He had trusted me and defended me without hesitation. In a moment, everyone stopped looking at me, and I could breathe again. What if I had made a mistake? Was that possible? I couldn't imagine how. But where was the buoy? There was no signal anywhere.

"Rock, sir. 10-and-7." Said Orta, who was on the lookout for asteroids. Although ships could sometimes be confused with asteroids, most of the time the rocks had a particular signature. When crossing a belt, there was always a man on the special scanner fixed on Level 7 probes used to find them. This time it was Orta.

"Rock. 10-and-7." Repeated Zell, out loud.

"Compensate starboard." Said the Captain.

"Yes, sir." Said Tumm.

The *Magnar* continued on course for a while, to where my calculations indicated would be the second buoy. But… nothing. Nothing was there.

"Mr.Iddo?" asked the Admiral.

"Still nothing, sir."

"Are we in the right place? What does the PTS say?"

Tumm, in Navigation, turned to junior officer Rumens, who was in charge of the Pulsar Triangulation System. Pulsars have very stable positions, so they're perfect as navigation references.

"We're in the right place, sir." Relayed Mr.Tumm.

"So where the hell is the damn buoy?" The Admiral got up from his chair.

I couldn't answer that question. No one could. I heard someone whispering something in the back and realized Mr.Orrey must be conferencing through the closed channel with the Captain and the Admiral. This went on for a few minutes. Finally, Captain Simmas ordered:

"Mr.Tumm, full speed ahead towards the third buoy, if you please."

"Sir!"

"Mr.Zell, report any contact whatsoever, please."

"Sir!"

I couldn't understand that last order. It was not a custom for the Captain to give redundant orders and that was obviously a redundant order. I had my eyes glued to the screens and my ears wide open to the head set. Of course, I would report any contact. What was that all about, anyway? Maybe they didn't trust me. Maybe they wanted Zell to check the sensors as well. But he didn't seem to be looking at the console. He was looking out into space, deep in his thoughts. And a quick glance showed me the Admiral and the Captain frowning, worried. What were they expecting? Suddenly, I got it. They were expecting foul play. They were expecting to learn that someone had been destroying, dislocating or stealing the buoys. The Silent, that is… They were expecting the Silent. This was a battle! Declared or not, we were at war already!

"Rock." Said Orta. "12-and-1."

"Rock." Repeated Zell. "12-and-1."

"Compensate port." Said the Captain.

"Yes, sir." Said Tumm. "Compensate port."

A green blink on my console!

"Contact!" I shouted. "Navigation buoy number 3! 1-and-2, sir!" (Meaning forward-right-high).

"Range?" asked the Captain.

"20-measures, sir!"

"Navigation?"

"We'll reach it inside an hour, sir," Tumm responded.

"When's the next batch due, Mr.Zell?" asked the First Officer.

"122 minutes, sir."

A ship can't launch probes in the middle of a fight. If a fight prolongs too much beyond the deadline for a probe batch launch, the ship could become long-distance blind very quickly. And a few minutes before the deadline the probe net would be already beneath 100% capacity, as some probes would already have dropped back and out. But if a batch was launched too close to the moment of contact with the enemy, the probes might not have time to lock in their paths before the ship started its combat maneuvers and might get lost in the process, escaping into deep space or even crashing against other probes or other obstacles. And the enemy didn't have the habit of announcing when it was coming into contact…

Then…

"Sir!" I shouted. "I've just lost contact, sir! The buoy! I don't have a signal anymore!"

Whispers filled the bridge. The Captain ordered:

"Mr.Tumm, set course for the fourth buoy, please. Full speed."

"Sir!"

And then the Admiral:

"Mr.Zell, send a signal to the fleet, if you please. Get me the destroyers' and frigates' probe report, on the double."

"Sir!"

After a couple of minutes, Zell reported back.

"The *Orink* and the *Dolymph* have the lowest count, sir. 61 and 69. All the others are above 100."

"Very well. Signal the *Kark*, the *Lion*, the *Carba* and the *Friel* to go ahead at full speed and find the fourth buoy. Tell them to clear the boards as they do so and exercise caution."

"Yes, sir," responded Zell.

Destroyers and frigates were much quicker than tier-one warships, so the Admiral was sending them ahead on a hunt. I felt cold sweat. This was exciting. This was a battle!

"The *Lion* is asking for ROE, sir." Said Zell.

"Free to engage, Mr. Zell." Answered the Admiral. He was not kidding around.

"Free to engage, yes sir."

"They're not going to play with us on this side of the Mirox, that's for sure."

I looked at Orta, he looked at me. The Admiral had given the order to engage. He was not kidding around! The whole bridge seemed to burst into excited whispers.

"BE QUIET, MEN!" shouted the First Officer. "This is the Admiral's bridge!"

We were supposed to be examples. We were supposed to be disciplined men. I forced myself to look at my screen. This was a battle! The system had been at peace for 60 years! And now we were at battle! War was coming! The older officers would have been in the Pirate Wars, but if the Admiral was right and the Silent came from Axx, well... these were no pirates...

*

The next couple of hours were tense. The fleet kept moving towards the sun and the fourth buoy.

"Signal from the *Lion*, sir." Started Zell.

"Go ahead." Said the Admiral.

"They reached the buoy, sir. It's exactly where it's supposed to be. No other contacts, sir."

"Ok," nodded the Admiral. "Tell them to launch an extra batch and keep the boards clear. How much time until we reach them, Mr.Tumm?"

"About an hour, sir."

"Very well."

The whole bridge had entered a special focus of some kind where no one seemed to be distracted by anything. Everyone was there, present, going about their tasks in a quiet, confident manner.

"Probes, Mr. Iddo?" asked Mr. Zell.

"Probes ready, sir. Launch in 20."

"Proceed."

Zell looked up, to the Constellation, and I followed his eyes for a second. The fleet was cruising in a diminished 'spine formation,' with the three big battleships in the center, one behind the other, and the bulky *Warhog* and the discreet *Pleeto* a bit lower in the back. The *Orink* was a bit behind and starboard, closing the formation, and the *Dolymph*, a frigate, was 'on point,' up ahead, along with the *Syrius*.

I looked at my console and announced:

"Probe launch in 10-9-8-7-6-5-4-3-2-1. Launch."

We felt a slight vibration going through the ship, as dozens of probes left their launch tubes and found their way into deep space.

"Rock." Said Orta. "11-and-8."

"Rock." Repeated Zell. "11-and-8."

"Compensate starboard." Said the Captain.

"Yes, sir." Said Tumm.

"Mr.Zell." Then started the Admiral. "Please ask the

*Dolymph* and the *Syrius* to keep inside the circle, if you don't mind. Let's not widen the formation too much."

(Orange light!)

"Yes, s…"

"CONTACT!" I shouted. "Level 9! 9-and-10!" (Left and high!)

Everyone seemed to jump in their seats. Everything got quiet for half a second.

"Image?" asked Zell.

"No image, sir."

"Where's she heading?" asked Orrey.

"No vector, sir."

"Clear the boards!" ordered the Captain.

And suddenly, everyone seemed to be speaking to someone else and doing something urgent.

"On the MID, if you please, Mr.Iddo," asked the Admiral, behind me.

"Sir!"

I sent the signal to the mimic display. But then…

"Contact! Level 8! 9-and-9! No image, sir!"

Everyone looked out there, to the signal. I heard the Admiral whispering:

"What's he doing?"

But we only had to wait a couple of minutes. Then I was shouting again.

"Red flag! Level 7! 8-and-8, sir!"

The Silent was approaching and quickly descending towards our bellies and backs. I could almost see the Admiral frowning behind me, trying to figure out the enemy captain's move. He said quietly:

"She's coming for a fight. Put them to work, Captain."

"Battle stations!" shouted the Captain. "Get all odds ready, Mr.Vallard!"

"Sir!"

"Quickly, Captain. Quickly." Said the Admiral.

"20-degrees port, Mr.Tumm!" ordered the Captain.

"Battle speed, if you please!"

"Sir! Battle speed!"

"Rock!" Called Orta. "1-and-5!"

"Ignore it!" Said the Captain. "Keep turning!"

"Mr.Zell, the *Dolymph* and the *Syrius* to circle port. On the double." Said the Admiral.

"Sir!"

Through the Constellation, I could see the *Magnar* leaning left and speeding up, although the gravity controls made us believe it continued straight and slow.

"Contact! Level 7! 8-and-7!"

"I don't think she's coming for us." I heard First Officer Orrey say. The Silent was still getting back and lowering the horizon.

"DAMMIT, MR.VALLARD!" shouted the Captain. "WHERE ARE MY WEAPONS?"

"All odds ready, SIR!!" responded the W-Comm.

I looked at the Constellation. The fleet was now getting in a line, gaining speed and curving to the left. All ships were battle ready. Only the *Dolymph* and the *Syrius* were far to the right, out of the Constellation display.

"Get us a target, if you please, Mr.Iddo." Said the Admiral.

"Doing my best, sir!"

I looked at my console, scanned the probes. Nothing. Where was she? There!

"Level 5! 8-and-7, sir!!"

"She's heading astern, sir!" said Orrey. "She's going for the butt."

"She's going for the *Warhog*." Said the Admiral.

The supply ship! Of course! Without a supply ship, the fleet could never get to Torrance. It would have to turn back. But the butt of the fleet... The *Orink* was back there! Lara was back there!

"Get me a vector, Mr.Iddo!" said the Captain. "I need a solution!"

I looked at the Constellation. The *Orink* was on the starboard side of the fleet. On the other side of the *Warhog*. So far, away from the threat.

"MR.IDDO! VECTOR!"

"No image, Captain! Only a blink! Too fast for triangulation, sir!"

"She's at Level 5, Dammit! How close must she get?"

"The last batch didn't lock, sir! We're not at full capacity!"

"Then tighten the levels, lieutenant! Get me a vector!"

"Just keep turning, Captain, keep turning." said the Admiral. "Mr.Zell, do we have the *Dolymph* and the *Syrius*?"

"4-and-3, sir! Heading right for us."

"Tell them not to wait for orders. Just attack. Clear us from the top, get to the target and attack!"

"Sir!"

"Mr.Orta," called Orrey. "Keep looking for rocks, if you don't mind. We wouldn't want to be crashing against an asteroid at this point, would we?"

"Sir! All clear, sir!"

And I shouted again:

"Level 4! 7-and-7, sir!"

"She's diving fast." Said the Admiral.

"Mr.Tumm!" called the Captain. "20-degrees port, 30-degrees-down. Let's get our bow deep, if you please!"

"Sir!"

"We're going to lose her." Said the Admiral. "She's going to get us before we circle."

And then Orrey:

"We need the *Orink*, sir."

My heart missed a beat. The *Orink*... But Admiral Hedde still had some ideas.

"Captain, fire blind." He ordered.

"Mr.Vallard, blind solutions. All odds, two tubes per battery." Said the Captain. "As close as you can to that red flag, please! Half a measure forward."

33

"Sir! All odds ready, sir!"

"Fire!"

"Fire!"

The whole ship trembled as 120 HCHE missiles left their tubes in odd hulls 1 to 11. We looked to the left and saw the white tails of the missiles as they traveled towards the black space.

"The *Viker* is firing as well, sir." Said Zell. "Blind solutions."

I looked back and saw the *Viker* firing and the tails of white smoke flying at 75,000 miles an hour towards the empty space.

"The *Taurus* is firing, sir." Said Zell. "Blind solutions."

We couldn't even see the tails of our missiles anymore, and then we lost sight of *Viker*'s and *Taurus*.' And then the explosions, far away. A series of small orange balls of fire surging here and there. But the area was too large. At this speed, the area got too large. The last missiles hadn't even exploded yet, and the Admiral was already issuing the order.

"Mr.Zell, signal to Captain Turrell that the *Orink* must get in there. Protect the *Warhog* at any cost."

"Sir!"

At any cost. No... Lara... And I looked at the Constellation and saw that the *Orink* was already moving, not waiting for orders, just speeding up and heading for the *Warhog* almost as if she was going to ram her or board her. And then I saw it. The sign. The warning sign. In my panel. I shouted.

"TORPEDO!"

'Torpedoes' are missiles that are at first propelled by invisible gas and laser catalysts until they are close enough to the target, undetected, and then they'll fire up the engines to accelerate and zero in and make sure the target doesn't escape. And they are powerful. Very powerful.

"Dammit!" Said the Captain.

"Torpedo! Another one, sir!! Heading for the *Warhog*,

sir!!"

"What's the *Orink* doing?" Said Orrey.

The past few hours had been amazing. Incredible. Literally incredible. As if I was watching some big special effects movie somewhere. Maybe in my mother's couch, laughing loud with my friends, drinking soda and eating chips and popcorn. Like I wasn't there, living all these exciting, scary adventures. Like the danger was somewhat of a joke some big clown was playing on us. The last few hours had been something of a blur. I moved as I was trained. I called it as I was trained. It felt unreal. But nothing as amazing as what happened then, in the next few seconds. A sight I would never be able to erase from my head. Everything like a dream. An amazing dream. A bad dream.

The *Orink* made the most incredible maneuver I would ever see in all my years in space. Incredible. Incredibly dangerous. Incredibly bold. Incredibly suicidal. The 50-battery destroyer was about to hit the *Warhog*, and then she climbed and… she rolled. Like a fighter-jet. She just rolled. And she over passed the supply ship from above, and… offered her belly to the torpedoes.

No sound is carried in space. But I heard the first explosion. Deep inside my mind, it went like the loudest bang, snapping my brain in. My mouth was open. My eyes hurt. The fire was burning holes in my irises. It was obvious to all of us that the *Orink* lost hundreds of people just on that first explosion. And there were immediately more explosions, secondary, of fuel or ammunitions exploding. Whole pieces of the ship were being torn apart.

*Lara…*

And then the other torpedo hit her.

*Lara…*

It was a fatal hit. We knew it was a fatal hit. I knew it was a fatal hit. The destroyer was unrecognizable. There were more explosions. She was breaking apart. Breaking in half. I couldn't believe it. We could see bodies of people being thrown into space, many of them with flames that extinguished almost immediately. All of them dead or dying in seconds.

*Lara...*

I couldn't see blonde hair. I tried to spot it, spot it in any of the bodies, but it was too difficult to see, too far, too fast.

*Lara...*

"That's it." Said the Admiral. "Burn the probes."

I couldn't believe what I was seeing. What I was feeling. I couldn't believe I was there, seeing it. I couldn't believe Lara was there, living it.

"Mr.Iddo!" Called Zell. "Burn the probes. Now."

I think I said: "Sir!" My hand moved on its own. It lifted the protection, and it pressed the button. And then the light. The bright light. And then black.

'Burning the probes' was a desperate move. It meant blowing all probes in a flash of white light that illuminated an immense area. Like the flash of a camera. The probes would be useless afterward, and the ship would be medium-to-long-distance blind until new probes were deployed, but for a split second everything illuminated by the light would be 'visible' to the ship's sensors.

For a split second, the virtual environment around us shut down so we wouldn't be blinded by the bright light. All went black. But then it switched on again. And she was still there. The *Orink*. Disintegrating. No survivors. Not for long. Not long enough. They would all die. No hope.

*Lara...*

"CONTACT!" I heard myself shout, my eyes mechanically looking at my screen. There it was. The Silent. The image of the Silent, the slick dark boat. The killer. The murdering bitch. Preparing to fire again. Finally uncovered.

"SOLUTION!" Shouted Weapons.

"ALL ODDS FIRE!"

"ALL ODDS FIRE!"

And then the whole Universe vibrated violently with the echoes of 500 missiles roaring through their tubes and jumping into action. The tails of white smoke blocking the field of vision.

"The *Viker* is firing. The Taurus is firing, sir!" Said Zell.

I couldn't see the *Orink*. I couldn't see it anymore. And then the missiles got further away, and I could see it again. And the missiles started to explode, and we saw the Silent with our own eyes, finally, and she was exploding. And the *Orink* took another torpedo, a last torpedo, and exploded even more, surprisingly, the wreck exploded even more. And the Silent exploded. Big, huge explosions of hundreds of missiles hitting their target. Her death very quick. Much quicker than the *Orink's*. Much quicker than Lara's.

*Lara…*

"Target destroyed, sir…" I whispered.

Looking back, I remember no one celebrated. Not on that bridge. We must have been all in shock. All looking at our colleagues, our comrades, and friends… and lovers, losing their lives in a terrible… unbelievable… hell.

"Did the Taurus and the *Viker* have their probes burned as well, Mr.Zell?" The Admiral seems to have asked.

"Yes, sir."

"Then tell the *Dolymph* she's the eyes of the fleet, now, if you please."

"Yes, sir. I beg your pardon, sir, shouldn't we…?"

"There won't be any survivors, Mr.Zell, but please signal the *Pleeto* and the *Syrius* to have a look."

"Yes, sir."

*Useless… It's useless…*

\*

There were no survivors from the *Orink*.

It had been a brilliant trap. Carefully planned and

executed. The Silent had lured the destroyers and frigates away with the buoys' distraction. And then attacked the weakest point in the fleet. The supply ship. Without all those supplies, the fleet would never reach Torrance. Would never project its strength and its image on the side of Torrance. Would not be in the way of the first wave of Axx attacks on the Kingdom.

In the end, it succeeded.

*

Commander Zell told me to sit opposite his desk and explained it to me.

"We're turning back, Mr.Iddo. We're not going to Torrance. The Navy still can't believe the 2nd Fleet almost got beat by a single Silent Boat. The Admirals are astounded. And the President thinks it's too dangerous to let the fleet go into the inner solar system, now. We would be sucked into a war we clearly are not prepared for. So we're turning back."

"Then we lost the battle, sir?" I was stunned. Lara had died for nothing. The *Orink* had been lost for nothing.

Mr.Zell sat back in his chair.

"To be honest, Mr.Iddo, I'm not sure. The consequences of what happened will take some time to sink in. I don't think we can keep looking at the war and the Navy the same way we were. We can't assume we have the most powerful ships in the system anymore. Not if they're close to useless against these Silent."

"But Torrance…"

"Torrance will have our help, don't doubt it, Mr.Iddo. Webbur will figure out a way to help it. It must. But for now, the fleet is keeping out of danger."

I didn't know what to say. I sat back and lowered my eyes to the floor.

"I know you had friends on the *Orink*." He said.

I looked up.

"I also had a lot of friends there. And I will miss them. But be sure of one thing, lieutenant…"

He hesitated.

"What, sir?" I whispered.

"Many more will die before this is over."

And he was right. Before it was over… I would just lose count.

But I would never forget Lara.

\*

Later on, I found myself lying on my bunk. My thoughts were stubbornly returning to the same images. Lara, the *Orink,* the explosions. I felt numb and drowning. Gaddy, from the T's, got in and I think he looked at me. Maybe he wanted to say something. But he didn't. He went to his bunk and left me alone. Left me staring into nothing.

Then, there was a whistle. I looked at the yellow plate of the loudspeaker on the ceiling.

"Hands of the *Magnar,*" it called with a familiar voice. "This is Admiral Hedde speaking."

Throughout the ship, everyone would be looking at a yellow plate.

"My friends, the last few hours have been surprising for many of us. For long we have been training together, and I know you all personally. Some better than others, but be sure I know you all. Through all the training we did, all the service we paid, I can with no doubt in my mind consider us, Webbur's 2nd Fleet, the most well-trained fighting force in the Universe. But for all our training, I know that most of us, maybe all of us, were not prepared for the pain and loss we have experienced. We all had friends and family in the *Orink.* We all had promises of good moments, of smiles, of love, of support and friendship. What we now have is pain. Is loss. But also memories. And those are the ones we should keep and cherish to guide us through our paths in the dark.

"And paths in the dark we will have. We were brutally and treacherously attacked and be sure we will be again in the future. We are heading to war. Maybe not right now, but be sure it will be there further ahead. So stand firm. And stay together. Cherish our good moments and our memories together. Hang on to our excellent training and our excellent comrades standing at our sides. And we will defeat the beast. With the certainty of destiny. Thank you all."

And the loudspeaker got quiet.

*Thank you, sir.* I thought.

I closed my eyes. I felt a single tear form and slip through the side of my eye. The cold and wet drop reaching my ear, uncomfortably.

And I wiped it off.

And I turned to the side.

And I fell asleep.

# EPISODE 2 – THE CONVOY

A sailor woke me up.

"Sir. Sir. We're here, sir."

I looked up, nodded and closed my eyes for two more seconds. When I opened them again, I was ready to go. I picked up my bag, loosen my seat belt and slid from the seat, holding myself to the handles on the walls. The shuttle was too small to have gravity controls, so I glided through the aisle until I found the airlock exit.

In seconds I was aboard the *W.S.Harvy,* where the 1G gravity allowed me to walk with heavy steps through the narrow corridors, ignoring almost everybody who couldn't tell me where my cabin was. I opened the small door and looked inside. A tiny cabin. But it was mine alone and these days that was as good as gold. I threw my bag into a corner, sat on the bed, against the wall and held my face in my hands for a while. I hadn't been sleeping lately. Not for a while. Not since the *Orink*-incident, as they called it.

"Hi."

I looked up. She must have been just 26 or 27. Five or six years older than me. She was leaning against the door, in her slim, well-built figure, her hands in her overalls' pockets, smiling peacefully as if she was strolling along in the countryside. Her long blond curls pinned behind her head. Her slender face and almost wide mouth accommodating an exquisite straight nose. And her green-gray eyes gazing as smooth as silk.

"I'm Mirany Cavo."

Startled, I jumped into attention.

"Sir!"

*

Admiral Hedde himself had called me on the *Magnar,* a few weeks ago. I had climbed the escalator to the C-Team HQ and had been introduced into his office.

"Mr.Iddo, we're going to lose you, I'm afraid."

My heart sunk even lower than it already was. He continued.

"It is vital we keep open the flow of goods into Torrance through the Dark Sea. Without it, our ally cannot resist. This means a lot of dangerous trips by our supply ships across the Sea."

He blew his nose in a feather-handkerchief.

"You know better than most how dangerous the trips are going to be. Silent Boats will definitely prey on the convoys, either Torrance's or ours. They will make a sailors' life a living hell, you can be sure of that. So the Navy has been recruiting a major supply fleet, getting good sailors from the civilian side. They won't be exactly Navy, not exactly military, but not exactly civilian either. Of course, we won't be able to protect everyone. The 2nd Fleet won't be able to be everywhere and probably won't be cruising too far from the Mirox. And we can't engage beyond the Mirox if not fired upon. We're still not at war. So you can see how dangerous this will be for the convoys for a good part of the journey, isn't that so?"

"Yes, sir" I almost whispered.

"And so they are asking for officers, Navy officers, warriors, who can integrate the convoys and help them pull through. We're sparing everyone we can."

Merchant fleet... I couldn't believe it.

"You'll be placed on the *Harvy*. As First Officer. She's led by the daughter of a friend of mine, you might have heard of him, Admiral Vincenz Cavo?"

Of course, I had heard the name, but this was even worst. I was being led by a woman! There were women in the Navy, certainly. Many of the *Magnar's* crew members were women. But the Navy didn't want them on the Towers. The command towers were, so to speak, a boys' club. There were no women First Officers, Captains and certainly not women Admirals. I had never thought much of the subject. The Navy was my home and whatever she decided was fine by me. But recent events had taught me different. As far as I was concerned, women did not belong in the Navy. They should be home. On solid ground. Making sure we had where to return to. Safe.

But I wasn't to be in the Navy. I was to be in Merchant fleet, and for them 'anything goes.' I was being demoted. I didn't know why, but I was being demoted and punished.

"This is neither a demotion nor a punishment, Mr.Iddo." said the Admiral. "You won't leave the Navy. You're a Navy officer, and this is what the Navy needs you to do, and for sure it won't be an easy job. Is that clear?"

"Yes, sir."

*

"Can I come in?" asked Captain Mirany Cavo at the door of my cabin. I was still in attention.

"Yes, sir."

With her hands in her pockets, she came in and sat on a lonely chair. She crossed her long legs.

"At ease, Mr.Iddo. Sit down."

I sat on the bed, again.

"You come from the *Magnar,* right?"

"Yes, sir. Signals' junior officer, sir."

"Big change, then."

"Yes, sir."

"You're not one of those who thinks being here is a demotion or a punishment, are you, Mr.Iddo?"

I probably turned red as a tomato.

"No, sir."

"We're all experienced space-sailors here, Mr.Iddo." She still showed the nicest smile. "We all have crossed the Dark Sea dozens of times, and we know the way to Torrance and back. What we don't know is how to fight an organized military navy. What we don't have is military experience or training. That's why we need you. "

"Yes, sir."

"Some of the boys and girls don't understand the nature of the game we'll be playing and think you're just here to make sure we're loyal. To check on us. But I think differently. I think we're going to have Silent Boats all over us and that this will be a long and bloody war, declared or not. What do you think?"

"I agree, sir."

"Can you help us against the Silent, Mr.Iddo?"

For a moment, I didn't know what to say. I didn't think anyone could help them against the Silent. They were sitting ducks. All they seemed to have was a herd advantage: the Silent simply wouldn't be able to kill them all. Kill us all.

"I'll do my best, sir."

She looked at me for a moment. Judging me. Then she got up, her hands in her pockets. Turning to leave.

"Welcome aboard, First Officer."

"Thank you, sir."

She smiled.

"And don't call me 'sir.' 'Captain' will do."

"Yes, s… Captain."

And she strolled away. Her hands in her pockets.

\*

The *Harvy* was a 700,000 tons cargo ship, probably built in the low gravity shipyards of the Brury moon. She was operated by a crew of 250 men and women. This time, she was filled with food, industrial glass, and *tyrium* containers, a material Torrance would need for probe manufacturing.

There was a stark contrast between the disciplined high tech hallways of the *Magnar* and the stoic narrow corridors of the *Harvy*. Most crew members smiled at me and were kind, but no one stood into attention nor carried a spotless uniform. Otherwise, the ship was indeed clean and organized for the most part. There was an air of excitement on board, but also of worry.

The Main Bridge was totally different from the one Admiral Hedde used to control the 2nd Fleet. The C-Tower was on the protruding bow. The bridge was on top and didn't have a hi-tech virtual environment as the *Magnar* did. Instead, it had large space-armored-glass windows all around and several screens, showing the scans from the surrounding space.

On each side of the Captain's and the First Officer's chairs were two descending steel vertical automatic stairs, leading towards the lower observation post, where one could look at the belly of the ship. I couldn't imagine, at this point, the number of times I would be forced to climb up and down those stairs.

Six people worked in the bridge. Most of them, women. Captain Mirany Cavo gave me a warm smile as I came in. I saluted her, and she smiled even more, taking a finger to her forehead in a relaxed gesture.

"Mr.Iddo, welcome to my bridge." She leaned against her seat, her hands in her overalls´ pockets. "Let me introduce you to the team."

Loly was a small, maybe a bit ugly, girl with a funny smile. She was the Tech, the *Harvy's* version of the T-Comm. Her big black eyes looked at everything at once, and she could muster any machine you'd like.

Zhany was a stark, beautiful brunette in charge of signals and sensors. She didn't speak much, but you would listen carefully to everything she said. She had a beautiful voice too, and I got to know many sailors who were hopelessly in love with her even without having ever seen her.

Krytia was tall, dark, wide shoulders, had a notable big nose and intelligent eyes. She was the 'Q,' handled Logistics and nothing was ever too perfect for her, even though she had a pleasant way to work it out.

And finally Rock, the pilot, a sixty-something white hair white bearded man, with wisdom beyond his years and not too keen to talk about it.

They all greeted me with nods or smiles. And then the Captain said:

"Would you please show Mr.Iddo how your stations work? We have about half an hour before we leave."

"We leave for what, s… Captain?" I wondered.

"We have a meeting at the *Ascim,* Mr.Iddo." She pointed towards a destroyer we could see at 10-o'clock through the window. "She's the head protection of the convoy. Her Captain will brief everyone about the trip, and I want us both there. You're very 'Navy-like,' so they'll respond better to you. And I want you to tell me what they'll be up to as well, of course."

*

The main deck of the *W.S.Ascim,* a 58-battery destroyer, allowed a big enough space for a meeting of several hundred people to take place. At this time, there were only a few dozen, mingling in the room while waiting for Captain Saltz, the Navy Captain commanding the ship and the actual leader of the convoy, to begin his speech. I came in with Mirany Cavo, and of course, everyone looked at us. She not only was the prettiest person in the room,she was also one of the most respected, as I soon found out. She introduced me to some of the captains of the other merchants, and I left her in the center of an admiring group to join a few Navy officers in a corner.

"Tym, with the T's." I greeted.

Young Gatty looked at me and smiled honestly.

"Hi, Byl."

"So, you've been attached to the cows as well."

"Aboard *W.S.Farcot,* a 900k." He kept smiling. "It's an important mission."

He actually meant it.

"Indeed."

He introduced me to the other officers, all juniors attached to merchants. There were 12 of us, placed in the biggest higher-risk ships in the convoy. As it turned out, I was the most senior of all. That shamed me a little, to be honest, as it meant I was the oldest of the 'Expendables' and so, potentially, the least talented of my generation. But I also felt responsible. It was easy to see that the lot of them was looking up to me, to be fair.

"Well," I said. "Be careful out there. If I'm not mistaken, it won't be an easy ride."

"That's just it." Said Gatty. "We don't really know what to do if we're attacked. What should we do?"

I looked at each of them. They all had a kind of troubled young look, as if somebody had forgotten to tell them to bring their books to school. But I knew what they were feeling. They felt like lambs to the slaughter, and if they had been briefed as thorough as I had, they hadn't been briefed at all.

"When it happens, just keep calm and remember your training. If your captains ask your advice, tell them to disperse from the convoy as soon as possible."

They were surprised. That was not the official Navy procedure for dealing with the Silent. But I couldn't see any better way.

At that point, Captain Saltz, a large sullen man, took to his stage and waited for everyone to be quiet. The crowd turned to listen, sitting on the available chairs. I saw Captain Cavo looking at me and understood she wanted me by her side, so I went, saluting my Navy friends with a casual couple of fingers, like a senior officer.

"Good evening, gentlemen." Started Saltz, carelessly ignoring the women in the room. "Thank you for your presence. In a few hours, we will initiate the voyage towards Torrance. QC1 will be the first Webbur run supply convoy to cross the asteroid belts and the Dark Sea since the beginning of the war, so there is no way of knowing if we stand in any danger from Axx's forces. Still, the Navy considers this trip to be extremely dangerous."

I looked around. Everyone knew we were in danger, of course.

"At this very moment, the 2nd Fleet is clearing up the path through the Mirox asteroid belt, making sure all the navigation buoys are in place and that there are no surprises, so we'll be safe as far as the belt. After that, the Fleet will no longer protect us and will remain on this side of the Dark Sea."

"Why is that, Captain?" asked one of the merchant captains.

Saltz twitched his nose, displeased he was being interrupted. He cleared his throat and answered.

"Well, we are not at war, at the moment, and our government surely doesn't want to provoke any foreign power by sending the fleet into the Dark Sea."

The room filled with whisperings.

"*Provoike?*" said another merchant, with a deep West Hiron accent. "What d'you call leading a *cuunvoy* to supply one of the *faactionz* with military raw materials?"

Saltz raised an eyebrow.

"Gentlemen, please. If you don't mind, I would rather you placed all your questions after my... well... presentation."

The audience quieted down a little.

"We should be able to go to the port in Torrance in 7 weeks.Four of those weeks will be spent crossing unprotected space. So it is paramount that we maintain our discipline and our focus. Nothing else will stand between the convoy and disaster."

"*Duisaster?*" intervened the hiron once more. "I thought we *weire* not at war, Captain!"

Saltz ignored him.

"The Navy is considerably short of convoy protection vessels and means. So QC1 will be guarded by only 4 ships, including two frigates, the *W.S. Loghi* and the *W.S. Yital;* a Corvette, *W.S. Ehm;* and of course, the *Ascim.*»

I saw Mirany looking at me, maybe trying to understand how uncomfortable I was with what Saltz was saying, and I looked away, trying not to show how scared I really was. 4 ships to protect 40 merchants was as bad of a joke as I'd ever heard.

Saltz took a pointer and showed us a board with images of ships in formation.

"Certainly you have been sufficiently briefed individually on the use of convoys. Maybe some of you have already participated in one or two. Either way, so we are completely clear, and there are no doubts, I would like to go over the convoy tactic as it has been molded by war experience. The basic convoy is established via two parallel lines of merchant ships, meaning, in this case, two 20-ship lines navigating side by side. The speed will inevitably be set by the two forward ships, and any vessel unable to keep up with it, by any malfunction or damage, must immediately leave the convoy, so not to deter any of the others. The convoy will be protected by a destroyer up front, one frigate on each side and a corvette in the rear. In case of any laggards, the corvette or a frigate will stay behind to protect her or them. Any questions so far?"

"Yes," said someone I couldn't see. "What if there are more laggards than protectors?"

Saltz didn't give much thought to the question.

"Well, the convoy comes first, of course. But I will elaborate on that in the end, if you don't mind. Now, if attacked, the convoy will make a circular turn to the side of the attack. So if the attack comes from the larboard side, we'll turn larboard, and if it comes from the starboard side, we'll turn starboard. The resulting 'circle of wagons,' so to speak, will ensure that either the attacker will be encircled and at the mercy of all our weapons, or it will be on the outside with no safe path to penetrate the formation. In case the attack comes from directly above or below the convoy, this will always circle larboard. It is, however, paramount that the formation is maintained. Is that clear?"

I looked around. The captains were definitely concerned, but some had had experiences with convoys in the Pirate Wars and knew that for the most part, they worked. Saltz continued.

"I know it may seem we will have little protection from the enemy, especially if he is using Silent Boats. But we have some new secret weapons with us. Weapons that haven't even been distributed to the Navy's mighty fleets! I'm speaking of the PTL30 Disposable Flash Probe, that can be fired into the dark and create a one-time powerful light flash and use a rigorous multi-layer sensor that can detect even the tiniest reflection in a deep space environment. The device is able to decode the specter of light in an instant to separate the light of the stars from the tiniest reflection on an invisible hull of a Silent Boat. If detonated at a reasonable distance of an invisible threat, we believe it will be infallible in detecting it."

I raised my eyebrow. I'd heard of the PTL30, and it was

good news it was available to us. I wondered, though, what Saltz meant by 'reasonable distance.'

"And also we will have the MSS1 cluster-missile, able to separate into over 50 warheads and spread a set of high explosive detonations through a wide area, so even if we don't have a very clear idea of the position of the threat we can still fight back and contain it."

Again, I was pleased. And so were many of the others, murmuring between each other. I looked at Captain Cavo for a second and saw her sigh, skeptical, before lifting her head and asking loud enough to be heard:

"Will those weapons be made available to us all, Captain Saltz?"

Saltz twisted, uncomfortable.

"I'm afraid not, ma'am. These are... uh... for Navy use only. You need to be well trained in their use for either of them to be effective, and also the ships have to be adequately equipped."

The whispering got louder. This time, with discontent.

"But all four Navy vessels in the protection unit are fully armed with them, gentlemen." Tried Saltz. "That is more than enough!"

"More than *enuff* for exactly *whoot*, Captain!?" asked the hiron. "Your own *pruutection*?"

The protests were spawning throughout the room until Mirany Cavo called again. All got quiet and turned to her.

"One more question, Captain!" She raised her voice, leaning back in her chair with her hands in the overalls' pockets. "I suppose the Navy ships will be launching a probe net all the way through?"

"Yes, ma'am."

There was a little twist in Cavo's eyebrow, maybe signaling a whiff of irritation.

"Captain, I command a ship, just like you, so I would appreciate if you'd do me the courtesy of calling me 'Captain,' and not 'ma'am.'"

There were some faint laughs. Saltz swallowed, uncomfortable.

"Of course, ma'am... uh... Captain."

"Well, Captain Saltz, if you will be launching a probe net, can I assume that this net will cover the whole convoy?"

"I'm afraid not, ma'am... uh... Captain. We don't have enough probes for that unless the convoy travels at a much-diminished speed. And that would be costly in supplies and time, as well as presenting a different kind of danger. The best chance comes from crossing the Dark Sea as quickly as possible before we're detected."

This comment sent the protests over the top.

"We'll be completely blind!"

"It will be suicide!"

"*Muirder!* It will be *muirder!*"

"They're sending us to die!"

"Sitting ducks! Just sitting ducks!"

"Gentlemen! Gentlemen!" said Saltz, troubled. "We *WILL* protect you! You must trust us! The Navy has provided several of you with trained advisors who will be at your service in your ships, and we will be in the front line immediately countering any threat that comes about. This convoy is vital! Please, remain calm!"

But no-one believed him. No-one remained calm. Until Mirany Cavo got up. Her golden curls sliding down her shoulders. Her peaceful smile resting below her perfect nose. And she said, calmly:

"He's right, lads. This convoy is vital. And that's why they called us. And that's why they're paying us top money. And we knew that. So let's just bite the bullet, shall we? Thank you, Captain Saltz, for your presentation and your words. And your advisors, of course. The *Harvy* is ready presently, welcomes your protection and awaits your orders to depart."

Cavo turned around, her hands in her pockets.

"Shall we go, Mr.Iddo?"

We could hear a pin drop behind us as we left.

*

As we traveled back to the *Harvy,* seated side by side in the 0-gravity environment of the shuttle, Mirany Cavo asked:

"What did you think?"

I didn't know what to say.

"About what, Captain?"

She didn't like my avoidance. She smiled.

"I know that you're a Navy officer, Mr.Iddo, and you feel obligated to the Navy, but you're also the First Officer on the *Harvy,* and you have responsibilities towards the ship and crew. And me. It is your duty, actually your primary duty, to form and communicate an opinion on anything I ask and you must fulfill it. Agreed?"

I trembled inside.

"Yes, Captain."

"So tell me: what did you think about what happened in there?"

"Well, it's good news that we will have PTL30's and MSS1's available. They definitely seem to be improvements in our weapons against the Silent."

"And...?"

"And it's good that everyone seems aware of the challenge ahead and they all seem to be competent sailors."

"But...?"

I looked into her eyes. Her smart, strong, beautiful eyes.

"But I maintain the opinion I had before."

"Which is?"

I slightly waved my head.

"I think it will be tough."

She sighed.

"You think we'll be attacked?"

"Yes, Captain, I do."

"And we won't be able to fight them off."

"No, Captain, we won't."

She seated back, adjusted the seat belt and the back of her seat, and rested her hands in her pockets, looking out the window to the Qwindy moon and the convoy vessels in orbit.

"Thank you, Mr.Iddo." She said, finally.

And we were quiet for the rest of the trip.

\*

We launched soon after. In a long stretched convoy, navigating at high speed towards the cargo ports of Hewel, in Torrance, weeks away. And in the days after the launch, I was finally able to know the *Harvy* a little better.

50 people manned the C-Tower, from cooks to medics to engineers. And then each of the 10 hulls employed 20 people. Compared to the massive 15 thousand crew members of the *Magnar* it was a quiet little crew, even if the whole ship was more or less the size of a 1st tier warship. That meant that if you were near the bow of the *Harvy*, it was mostly silent. Only if you were close to the engines would you hear the constant drum of the machines.

I managed to get to know all of the hulls in the free time I had before we got to the Mirox. There was the usual autonomy of the hulls as well, which meant we actually had about 11 different crews on board. I liked them all, I have to say. They were usually efficient and direct but without the flair and determination of the Navy. Yet they did their jobs well. Nothing in the ship seemed out of order or out of place.

The walks also helped me relax a bit and avoid the depression I was finding in my cabin: I was still having trouble sleeping.

One interesting thing, in the Navy, we call the second in command of a ship a First Officer, an F.O. if in writing, or simple «number one», sometimes. Cavo had the courtesy of calling me First Officer on my first days aboard; however, in Merchant Navy, they call us Executive Officer or X.O. And that's the calling I inherited. After a few days, I was really starting to feel it: I was the *Harvy's* X.O.

After a few days into the voyage, I was also feeling something else: there was a lot of tension in the air. People were irritable and worried. More fierce discussions and arguments than usual seemed to break out and even though each hull-captain would deal with its own team's problems, the troubles in C-tower had to be handled by me and the master-of-the-tower, an angry looking old sailor called Verca. For the first time in my 4-year-old career in spaceships, we had a fight after only two days in Space. Something about somebody's socks, if you can believe it. Verca called me, but after he told me what was going on and I got it was only a small thing, I let him decide the matter. I didn't know anybody well enough to start passing judgment just yet. When the second fight broke out just the next day, Captain Cavo stepped in and made a speech over the intercom. It was a short, simple speech about danger, courage and the ability of the crew, but it worked. «I wouldn't be here with anybody else, would you? We're a solid team. So let's keep our heads cool and do our duty, shall we?» She said. Arguments seemed to disappear as of magic.

Captain Mirany Cavo was a constant surprise. She commanded tremendous respect from her crew. But she had a special way of going about it. Commanding, I mean. She was smoother, simpler, milder than any captain I had served with. And it would seem incredible to anyone in the Navy that she could ever discipline a crew in Space in this manner. But everyone always felt, well, privileged when she was around. Her smile made even the hardest of sailors blush like a little girl. Many just held their breaths when she walked by. And it wasn't like it was all seduction, nor were they all in love with her. But she always seemed to do the right thing. And she impressed people. Deeply. Like she impressed me. Like she impressed Captain Saltz and everyone else aboard the *Ascim.*

*

As we were a small C-Team, the usual shift on the bridge was just one or two strong. It suited me fine. Unlike the *Magnar's* bridge, so large that you would basically be on your own, in your station, with nobody really bothering you for hours, the *Harvy's* bridge was almost crowded with two or three people on it. So in the next few days after launch, after L-Day, I was happiest when I was alone, on the bridge, in a few hours' shift, and I went to the point of doing several four-hour shifts back to back, letting other people rest.

The lone shifts looking into deep space or the bleeps on the screens weren't as restful or as peaceful as before. Ghosts came rushing in. Ghosts of burnt bodies, cooked by fire, by pressure and radiation, floating in the void. Ghosts of ships exploding and torpedoes running. Ghosts of sweet eyes and soft words. Ghosts of love. Long gone love.

But still, nothing else smoothed my mind. Work made me realize the sour taste in my mouth. Sleep never came easily in my cabin. Walks helped, but they weren't too convenient. Only the bridge, looking outside, watching other ships in the distance, the sun, the stars, let me slide into some kind of numb meditation. Breathing in and breathing out.

To my surprise, after a few days into the voyage, Mirany Cavo started to come by, when I was alone. And she would stay for a while. A few hours even. The first day we exchanged some small talk and then settled into silence for a long time. It was strange, and it felt weary for a bit. But then it became comfortable. When she left, she took a finger to her forehead, smiled and said:

"You have the bridge, First Officer."

The second day we talked a bit longer. She asked me:

"Byllard Iddo... How do your friends call you? Byl? Lardy? 'Billiard Ball'?"

I almost laughed with her.

"Byl," I answered.

"Do you mind if I call you Byl? You can call me Mira when we're alone."

"Sure."

She kept surprising me. That was completely off protocol. It was the kind of exchange we would never have had in the Navy where the hierarchy was so obvious. A Captain would never be on first name basis. But she did call me Byl, and I did call her Mira. When we were alone. That day, when she left, she took a finger to her forehead, smiled and said:

"You have the bridge, X.O."

That small change didn't elude me. For the first time, I really felt I was a merchant. And for some reason, I didn't feel bad about it.

*

On the third day, I found myself almost anxious for her arrival. And I managed a smile when she came by. And we started talking almost immediately. And after a while, we started learning about one another.

"I had a little boat called *Ghendy*." She said, her smile wide and her eyes gazing into the outside void. "My grandfather gave it to me on my tenth birthday. I used to sail in the Olony Lake almost all year round. I would sail for hours almost every day. My mother worried, of course, but there was nothing she could do. After I grew up a little more, I started to sail in the summer nights."

She looked to the Space around us, comfortably.

"In the dark of the lake, the stars seemed my special companions. I invented names for each of them. Proper names, like Bary or Steev, not the star map names. That's when I decided to join the Navy. "

I followed her gaze and smiled a little as well. I knew what she meant. She looked at me and frowned a bit.

"I thought my father would be proud, but he wasn't. He actually forbade it."

She gave a little laugh.

"That was a mistake. For both of us. I ran away when I was 16 and joined the merchants. That was my mistake, I guess. You wouldn't believe how bad they can be to 16-year-old girls. I was lucky to have a good mentor, Captain Hay. Without her to protect me, I don't know…"

Her eyes said everything. It had been bad. She lifted her chin.

"When I was 17, my father found me and sponsored my entrance into the Space-Navy Academy. I graduated at 19."

So she had military training… Why had she…?

"So you were in the Navy?" I asked.

"Yes." She strokes her hair. "But when I said earlier that we needed assistance against an organized enemy, I was being honest. I'm not up-to-date on battle tactics and forgot most things I learned back there. I served only six months on a warship. Junior officer in a hull. But I knew the best I could hope for in the Navy was to be hull-captain, and I found that wasn't enough. So I left and looked for a command of my own in merchants. With my record, it wasn't difficult. I was a Captain when I was 21."

That was impressive. But I looked away, at a useless bleep on a screen, faking indifference. Why did I do that? Navy habits, maybe.

"How about you?" She then said. "How did you get into the Navy?"

I shrugged my shoulders.

"Nothing so romantic, I'm afraid."

A shadow crossed her eyes.

"My story? It didn't feel romantic at all to me, believe me."

I straightened up, uncomfortably.

"I know... I mean... I meant I didn't have a particular infatuation with the stars, growing up, like you did. Not until I joined the Navy, anyway. I did like ships, but... well..."

"You're from Riddario, right?"

"Yes. Vell Mountain, in fact. Yiggal Town. My mother had a furniture shop, and my father taught martial arts."

"No kidding? Which kind?"

"*Tzaido.* He was a master of *Tzaido.*"

"Did you practice?"

"Yes. Since I was 5."

"You don't look like the type, actually. No big muscles or anything."

"*Tzaido* is about speed and flexibility, not strength."

She stopped and looked at me from head to toe, for a moment. I think I might have blushed.

"But we're deviating." She smiled, beautifully. "Tell me how you enlisted."

"My father died when I was 16. My mother remarried and sold the *dojo*, and so, when I was 17, I left and joined the Navy. I just couldn't remain there."

She was surprised but recovered fast.

"I understand," she said.

"I was accepted into the Academy, and the Navy became my home. I never looked back."

I had never explained my journey in this manner, to someone I hardly knew. But even though I felt my heart tremble for a second, it actually had been much easier than I would have imagined. I just had to tell her. I had to tell her about the death of my father, I had to tell her about the rejection of my mother. I saw her looking at me, pretending to be relaxed but fully aware of the impact of this conversation.

"Do you still keep in touch with your mother?" She asked.

"Yes. We talk once in a while, and I visited a couple of times. She is divorced now."

"I'm sure she's glad to have you. Your enlisting must have been hard on her. And why haven't you joined the Marines or the Army? They would love someone with your background, I'm sure. Martial Arts, mountain boy. What made you join the Navy?"

"Exactly that, I guess. I didn't want to be in close quarter combat. Nor kill anyone. At least up close." Was I going too far too fast? Revealing too much? "And I wanted to know new planets and travel through Space, of course. And I did like ships."

She gave me a sad smile.

"I understand. *Tzaido* can be deadly, I hear."

"Yes. Yes, it can."

She turned in her chair, to make it easier to face me.

"Do you still practice?"

"I used to. On the *Magnar*. Two or three times a week, with a marine I know. But I haven't for a couple of months, now. Since…"

Ghosts came back in a wave, and I stopped abruptly. She must have seen me go pale and picked up the whole story in my face.

"Since the *Orink* incident?"

I looked up at her. She knew. She knew about it. But how much did she know exactly?

"Yes."

"What happened?"

I looked into her eyes. She didn't know everything. I had to be careful, here. I gave her the official version.

"One of her engines malfunctioned in the Mirox, and

she crashed into an asteroid. No one survived."

She blinked.

"That's what the papers say. The Navy's version."

I blinked back.

"It's what happened." I lied.

She sat back. She looked outside. The sun appeared from above, for a moment, after a tiny automatic change of course. It was a small ball of light far up ahead, in the dark heart of emptiness.

"I wanted to go back to the Navy, you know?" She said, lifting a blond curl from her eye. "When the war between Axx and Torrance started. When Torrance declared war. I wanted to go back. To be ready to fight. But my father was against it. He was afraid for me. And he threatened to stop me, call everyone he knew and stop me. And he would, you know? He is still powerful. So I said I'd volunteer. If there ever was to be a merchant convoy system to supply the *torries,* I'd volunteer. And he knew he wouldn't be able to stop that. So I asked him a favor. Both because I needed it and because it would calm him down."

I looked at her. Her eyes out there. A ray of light shaping her perfect profile. Her peaceful face slightly twitching with a streak of determination. And then she turned to me and looked me in the eyes. And I trembled again. She said:

"I asked him to get me some help. To get me a crew member, an outstanding First Officer, who would be smart, very competent, thought for himself, knew what he was doing, and, most of all, had experience in fighting Silent Boats."

I almost jumped. She smiled.

"I know you have been feeling neglected and punished for having been sent here to serve on a merchant ship. Not even a 1 million or a 900k, like some of your younger colleagues, but a 700k, even if it is a good one. Maybe you've even resented being commanded by a woman. But you're here because my dear father, a brilliant old Admiral, knows how to pick a good hand, and wanted to give me the best."

My heart stopped beating. What… What was she talking about? Was that true? Was she real? Had I been spotted and sponsored by a famous Admiral?

"So, you see?" She continued. "You must have experience fighting a Silent. That's what I asked for. And that's why I don't believe for a second that the *Orink* crashed against an asteroid."

Oh, she was so wonderful! So beautiful. So smart.

"But that means that a Silent dared to defy the 2nd Fleet on this side of the Dark Sea and managed to 'sink' a destroyer." Her smile died a little. "And you can be sure that that idea alone keeps me awake at night. And we're not the 2nd Fleet. Not by a long shot."

And then I said it. I don't know why I said it, maybe because at that moment she was as bright as a star. I don't even know what I meant by it, even though I felt I meant the world. But I had to say it. It just came out.

"That's ok," I said. "I'll be here when they come."

And I meant it. Like I knew what to do. Like I could save us somehow. And her eyes widened with surprise. And we stood there. For a moment. We stood there looking into each other's eyes. And she smiled that perfect smile. And then she sat back again, and looked away, with that peaceful look on her face and her smile still honestly lying there.

"Thank you, Byl." She said. "That means a lot."

I looked away as well. And we were in silence for a while. We watched the stars. Then, finally, she got up, she got closer, she put a hand on my arm. I felt so relaxed, suddenly. She smiled again.

"You have the bridge, X.O."

I smiled back, reassuringly.

"I have the bridge, Captain."

And then she left.

\*

A few days later we approached the Mirox asteroid belt. On the bridges of every ship in that convoy, the full C-teams were on station, alert against asteroids and other debris, maybe fearing the edge of the frontier, a possible close encounter with a deadly enemy. When the convoy reached the first navigation buoy, a special surprise was waiting. The whole 2nd Fleet, now 14-ship strong, was there on guard, seeing us through.

"The *Ascim* is issuing a general salute, Captain." Said Zhany.

The Captain nodded, sitting back in her high chair.

"We'll salute as we pass the flag." She said.

There they were. Several destroyers, two frigates, the supply ship, the repairer *W.S. Pleeto*, a new 74-battery 3rd class Warship, the *W.S.Benavide,* and the familiar heavyweights: the 90-battery 2nd class *W.S.Taurus* and the 70-battery 3rd class *W.S.Viker.* And finally, at the center of the formation, the massive *W.S.Magnar,* the 120-battery 1st class flagship. My old ship. Grey, red and green. Majestic.

"Salute the flag, Zhany."

Mirany looked at me. Maybe trying to decode my feelings. I was sitting straight in my chair, feeling homesick, ship-sick, but not really knowing if I'd rather be there or here (next to her – there was a strange little voice in the back of my head whispering «next to her»).

"Salute issued, Captain."

I avoided eye contact with Mirany. Focused on the fleet. On the *Magnar*. I really missed it.

"The *Magnar* returns the salute, Captain."

"Very well."

"They also sent a message to Lieutenant Iddo, Captain."

Zhany's words hit me like a rock. A good rock. This was off protocol. Now I looked at Mirany, a bit embarrassed.

She raised an eyebrow, in a movement I didn't really understand (Jealousy? Irritation? Curiosity?)

"Go on." She commanded.

"It's an encrypted message, Captain."

Mirany smiled.

"Just deliver it, Zhany."

Zhany looked at me, uncomfortable. I must have been completely stiff, my curiosity paralyzing every muscle. An encrypted message?

"It says YVNOK."

*YVNOK?* I must have looked puzzled because Zhany spelled it.

"Y-V-N-O-K, sir."

I knew what it was. It was a level 4 coded message. A simple substitution code we used in the Navy for very low-level messages. And I knew what it meant. Even without a key. Even without the *Magnar's* key (each ship had its own). It was a standard message. That only I would be able to recognize aboard the *Harvy*. It meant PRAYC. *Please Report At Your Convenience.*

I looked at Mirany. I was feeling quite peaceful suddenly, and I must have been smiling because she smiled me back. She said:

"You can reply, if you want, Mr.Iddo."

I knew what the message was saying. Admiral Hedde was telling me I could return whenever I wanted. He was reminding me I was still Navy. No matter where I went. No matter what happened. No matter which ship I was in... I could go back.

I turned to Zhany.

"Just acknowledge in my name, if you please, Zhany."

"Very well." She hit the keys in her console. "Acknowledged, X.O."

"Thank you, Zhany."

*

The passage through the Mirox, as it turned out, went on without incident. Soon we were navigating in the Dark Sea. The fleet had been left far behind, and we were now flying in convoy formation, two parallel lines, straight through the vast empty space.

Nothing really happens in the Dark Sea. There's nothing there. No planets, no moons, a few very isolated asteroids, no planemos, no dwarf planets, nothing. It's just empty space between two asteroid belts and two highly populated areas of the solar system. Theoretically, it should have been the safest place to travel. In practice, it was just the opposite.

*

Two days into the Dark Sea crossing. I was on the bridge with Zhany and Rock. Things were calm. The shift was going according to plan. We had a small glitch in Hull 6's gravity generator, which caused a bit of a fuss, but it was quickly resolved, and otherwise, nothing major was going on.

My attention was on the black void. A meditation of some kind. All my usual duties had been fulfilled, and now all I had to do was babysit the bridge. Not that it needed it, though. Zhany and Rock knew their jobs top to toe.

Zhany's console showed a blink. Some sort of a blink. And I happened to see it. I used to be Signals so... I didn't ignore it.

"Was that a warning, Zhany?"

Zhany looked at her screen.

"Well, if it was it's not there now, X.O. Probably a false."

Oh, no. That didn't do it for me. I approached her station.

"What was it?"

65

"It came from the *Loghi*, sir," She answered. "A relay from one of her probes. But it wasn't confirmed."

"What heading?"

"10 and 10."

"Level?"

"11."

*Loghi* was the escort frigate on the port flank. I looked to the left. Couldn't see her, of course.

"Ask them to confirm it," I ordered.

Zhany was taken aback.

"It was one blink, sir. I'm sure it was another false alarm."

I raised my eyebrow.

"Has it happened before?"

"A couple of times in the last 20 hours or so…"

Now I was worried.

"Ask the *Loghi* to confirm the contact."

"But X.O.…."

"Just do it, Zhany!"

"Yes, sir."

I looked at Rock. His face was troubled. I got back to my chair, opened a compartment next to it and took a pair of powerful electronic binoculars. The *Harvy* didn't have fancy sensors so many times these specially linked binoculars were the best we had to look around us. I put the strap around my neck and got back to Zhany.

"Show me the convoy on the primary display."

She did as she was told and I looked up at the large screen. The formation was linear and very steady. No one was reacting to the contact. I looked through the binoculars. With a touch of the fingers, I connected them to the onboard computer and asked to enhance the *Loghi's* position to the left. A circle of green light showed me the position of the frigate, a little dot of reflected light in the dark. I looked at 10-o'clock-high, 10-and-10, asking the binoculars to enhance any reflection close enough, but of course, they didn't pick up anything. I looked straight ahead. The Gera, a 500k merchant, was there. Her engines glowing, right in position. I went to the right-hand window and looked at our starboard side. Could see the *Sodah,* a 600k merchant, on our flank, close enough to see the bridge. Nothing was happening. But I wasn't at peace. Something was happening. I just knew it.

"The *Loghi* has confirmed a false alarm, X.O." Said Zhany.

I twisted my nose and slid down the metal stairs to the belly observatory. I used the binoculars to look towards the stern. I could see the *Farcot* right behind us, way back in position. And another ship behind it. The *Haarly.* Nothing else. The rear escort Corvette had been dispatched to help a laggard. But was anything else out there? Maybe I was exaggerating. Maybe the *Orink* incident got me to imagine things. I sighed and climbed the stairs back to the bridge. Both Rock and Zhany looked at me, concerned. Maybe because they thought I was wrong, and I was just going crazy. Maybe because they thought I was right, and something dangerous was out there. I looked at Zhany's screen.

"Any other blinks?"

"No, sir."

We watched the screen together for a while. Nothing.

"Probably a false." I conceded. I took the strap off my neck and sat back on my chair, the binoculars resting on my knees. I was thinking. It just took another five or six minutes.

"X.O.!" Zhany put the new contact on primary. 9 and 9, Level 9. It was there just for a second, but now I knew it wasn't a false.

"Call the Captain, Zhany. Get everybody up here."

She hit the keys. Rock looked at me, I looked at him.

"If it comes, Rock, we need to move fast."

Rock nodded. We were on the same page.

Mira took three minutes to get there. Kritia and Loly took two more. Kritia took the Weapons station, and Loly took the sensor screen from Zhany. I briefed them. There was a small concerned wrinkle in Mirany's forehead.

"Danger, X.O.?"

"Most likely, Captain."

She looked into my eyes and immediately believed me.

"Any ideas?"

"Not yet. She's going left and back. That's all we know. And nobody is reacting, which means they still think it's nothing. We asked the *Loghi* twice to confirm the contacts, but they didn't get it. Still mistrusting the probes."

"And that's a mistake, I gather?"

"I wouldn't, Captain."

"Ok."

We used our binoculars, trying to look everywhere. But it was too empty, too dark, and we had to be careful not to get sick. It was very easy with those binoculars. Even for experienced hands.

A few minutes passed. A few silent worried minutes. Mirany looked at me.

"What would you be doing if you were in the Navy, Mr.Iddo?"

Easy call. That answer I knew.

"I would be clearing the boards, Captain."

Mirany nodded.

"Zhany, issue a message to the whole convoy. The *Harvy* is clearing the boards."

There wasn't a Merchant Fleet equivalent to 'clearing the boards.' No boards to clear, in fact. But that message surely would not be ignored. In a few minutes, several merchant ships were responding. They were 'clearing the boards' as well. In seconds, the whole convoy was on alert status. The merchants trusted Mirany more than they trusted the Navy. And Mirany trusted me.

"Captain," Zhany called. "The *Ascim* is hailing! Captain

Saltz for…"

"CONTACT!!" shouted Loly.

"Fucking hell!" said Rock next to her, protecting his ear. I lashed at Loly.

"What's the heading?! Dammit, Loly, put it on primary!"

We all looked at the screen. Oh, hell! She was 6-and-9! Right behind us!

"BATTLE STATIONS!!" I shouted. But they looked at Mirany.

"Battle stations!" She called. "Battle stations everyone!"

Not quick enough!

"TORPEDO!" shouted Loly.

Oh, fuck! Mesmerized, we all looked at the primary screen. There it was. That slash from a brush of fire. That moving tail of white smoke and orange flame in the dark. That sign of death. It went on directly to the target. It passed one ship, then another…

"It's going for the *Farcot.*" Said Zhany.

"Oh, the stars help me…" said Kritia.

It was as if it was happening in slow motion. The *Farcot* was hit very close to the main engines, and there was an explosion, and for a moment it seemed much smaller than we would think. But just for a moment. Then the real explosions started to break it apart. One engine. Then another… The *Farcot.* Tym Gatty's ship. Breaking apart. I knew immediately he wouldn't survive. No one would.

"Oh, the stars help me …" Someone said.

I was the first to shake it off. To take my eyes off the screen. Off the balls of fire swelling in the dark. I looked for the Silent.

"She's moving in!" I said, gaining the Captain's attention. "She's pursuing the back merchants! She's going to get inside the convoy and use missiles!!"

"ANOTHER TORPEDO!!"

There it was: it was going to hit the *Farcot* once more. Just like the other time. More explosions!

Mira looked into my eyes. There was a question there. She didn't know what to do.

"Oh, poor souls…" said Kritia.

And then Mirany nodded.

"Act." She whispered. And I nodded back.

I jumped into my chair and fastened my seat belt while I ordered:

"Rock! Break left! Full speed! All the way port!!"

And Rock would hesitate. And he would look at Mirany to get her consent. But before that he obeyed. Just like he should. He just did what he was asked. Instinctively. Good man! The *Harvy* left the convoy formation and turned left. And then we got hit. We felt the impacts, the ship trembled, and then Kritia's screen started flashing red lights.

"We got hit!! We got hit!! We got hit!!"

"Where?" asked Mirany, fastening her seat belt.

"Hulls 7 and 5!"

"Missile fire?"

I knew it wasn't. Not violent enough.

"Debris," I answered. "*Farcot's* shrapnel!"

"Loly?"

Loly seemed to have tears in her eyes, but her voice was firm.

"No missile, Captain. It must have been debris!"

But in zero-gravity and that speed, debris could be just as dangerous.

"We have a breach, Captain! Hull 7!" Called Kritia. "And Bravo Engine got hit! I don't know if we can keep it!"

Mirany released herself and got up.

"Loly! With me! Kritia, you have Sensors! X.O., you have the bridge, I'm going back there!"

"I have the bridge!" I assumed it without the slightest hesitation like it was second nature to me. I even managed to nod to Mirany to assure her it was okay. *I have it.* And then she left. And Loly followed her.

"Missiles! Missiles! Missiles!" announced Kritia.

I looked at the primary. There she was. The Silent. Shooting at close range with her full 24 HCHE batteries. Hitting the *Haarly* and the *Dhofer* left and right, once and again, even before they could get their low-grade missile batteries in order. All 10 or 12 of them. And the explosions lighted the black. Hurt our eyes.

"Oh, the stars..." Said Kritia.

"The *Ascim* is hailing, sir." Said Zhany. "Captain Saltz demands we get back into formation!"

"Keep turning, Rock!" I ordered. "Lower the bow and turn hard! Get us out of the way of that bitch! Are the weapons ready, Kritia?"

"All even batteries ready, sir! And most of the odd! We don't have 5 nor 7!"

"Solutions?"

"Negative, sir. Not yet."

I picked up my binoculars and rotated my chair.

"Do I acknowledge the *Ascim*, sir?" asked Zhany.

"I'm busy!"

I looked to the rear. The *Haarly* was on fire. The *Dhofer* was on fire. The Silent was gaining speed and moving up the convoy. I looked at the primary screen. The *Loghi* was approaching rapidly to intercept the Silent. But the escort frigate wouldn't be getting any fire solution quick enough. None better than us. And she wouldn't be able to use the PTL30's or the MSS1's because the Silent was inside the formation and the cluster-missiles would hit the merchants just the same!

But the *Harvy* was getting out of the way. The *Harvy* was getting the tragic wreckage of the *Farcot* between herself and the enemy. The *Harvy* was going to survive.

"MISSILE LOCK!!"

Fuck! They got us!! Through the eye of the needle, they'd managed a solution.

"Missile!! Missile!! Missile!!"

"Wait for it!" I said. I looked at the distance measures.

We'd managed enough distance. The missiles were closing in. "Countermeasures, Kritia. Batteries 2 to 6. On my mark." I counted backwards. 3-2-1. "Release!!"

The countermeasures flew away. There was an explosion. We felt the shock waves hit us. The ship vibrated. And there was a soft bang, and I looked and saw a burned disfigured body bumping against the bridge's window and flying away. And then the gravity controls failed. Maybe it was shrapnel from the *Farcot* or the missiles, maybe it was just the shock. Rock was strapped, and so was I, and Kritia held on tight, but Zhany didn't have her seat belt on and flew off violently towards the ceiling. I managed to grab her foot just before she'd crash and break her head. I pulled her to me, and she looked at me, wide-eyed, scared stiff and nodded, and I pushed her towards her station.

"Strap yourself, Zhany."

"Yes, sir!"

There were no more missiles. I looked through my binoculars and saw the faint silhouette of the Silent pursuing the Gera.

"Zhany! Warning to the Gera. Enemy ship 6-and-9. Climb 90 degrees now!"

"Enemy ship 6-and-9. Climb 90 degrees now. Yes, sir!"

And the Gera started to climb, leaving formation. And the Silent followed her for a bit, leaving the convoy as well, looking for a solution. But the *Loghi* was approaching and preparing to fire. So the Silent vanished. It was there one minute and the next she was gone. Leaving behind nothing but fear and destruction.

\*

It took me about an hour to feel I could leave the bridge to Rock without much trouble, with gravity back to normal and everything under control. Mirany hadn't come back or checked in yet, and we weren't able to reach her. I went to find her and just bumped into her in the corridor.

"Byl."

"Mira."

She looked me in the eyes. She looked exhausted. Her hair was messy. She had a small cut on the side of her face and dirt all over her suit.

"Is everything okay?" She asked.

"The Silent's got four ships. Over 2.5 million tonnes. No survivors."

"But is everything okay?"

"Yes," I nodded. "We got away."

She sighed.

"Come with me."

She led me to her quarters. She pointed to the table, and I sat down. She picked up a bottle of *awrey*. Clear as ice and just as chilly. And two glasses. And she sat across me. And poured a couple of shots. We both drank them in one go, and then she poured some more.

"We had a breach... Worst than we thought." She said. "Lost five hands in Hull 7. And two more from the rescue party."

She drank again and poured again.

"Loly managed to close the hole, but then... At the last minute, she fell. Six meters. She broke her neck. And a lot more bones, I'd expect. She didn't make it."

I drank as well. I remembered Loly's weird smile. And Tym Gatty's timid eyes.

Mira's hand came across the table and took mine.

"Thank you." She said.

I squeezed her hand. And for a few minutes, we remained there. Looking at the empty wall. Breathing deeply of both sadness and relief. Hand in hand. Sweaty palm in sweaty palm.

"Come on." She said finally, releasing her fingers and getting up. "We have a wounded ship to run."

*

The next day, we were called to the *Ascim*. Mirany and I were escorted by a petty officer to the Captain's office where Saltz was sulking behind the desk. His First Officer stood next to him, with a grave face. Saltz greeted Mira with a melting handshake and responded my salute with a sloppy gesture, pointing to the chairs where we could seat.

"Please."

He then crossed his hands over the desk and looked at us both.

"I'm very disappointed in you. A military operation is a difficult and rigorous thing. It needs absolute discipline and alignment. We are traveling dangerous 'seas,' and there's a war going on. I was clear at the beginning of the journey. A convoy works in a very specific way, within specific rules. For everyone to have a better chance of survival, that's how it is. And the one thing that cannot happen, the one thing that can create a real mess of it all and put us all in danger is if each ship suddenly starts to decide what to do on her own."

Mirany was just sitting there really calm, listening to the man, but I was feeling uncomfortable, so I tried to speak.

"Sir, if I may…" I started.

"YOU CERTAINLY MAY NOT!!" He suddenly turned red, pointed his finger and shouted. "YOU ARE A NAVY OFFICER! YOU SHOULD HAVE KNOWN BETTER!!"

"Be careful, Captain."

Mirany's very calm but strict voice stopped him right there. We all looked at her. Saltz had a very surprised look on his face. Mira looked into his eyes and continued, a definite menace faintly carrying in her tone.

"We are not low-life moon-based scavengers on our first long-haul trip… You know why we are here. So please calm down."

Saltz's eyes opened wide, shocked, trying to figure out what was happening. I was also surprised and trying to grasp it. To this day I don't know if she was referring to the Admirals that had put us, her and me, in this convoy, our patrons, or to the clout she carried within the merchants, and some sort of idea that we were representing them all. But Captain Saltz immediately calmed down. He grabbed his own fingers.

"You... You disobeyed my orders in the battlefield. Several others followed you. That will not do."

"Yes, Captain, I understand." Smiled Mira. "But please understand that if we hadn't acted fast enough, we would have lost more ships. The *Harvy* would've certainly been lost. And that was unacceptable. We were in a better position to perceive the whole situation, so we acted. Can we agree on that?"

Saltz didn't say a word. He uncomfortably looked at her.

"Now..." said Mira. "Would you please listen to what my Executive Officer has to say?"

Nothing, for a few moments, but then he nodded.

"Please speak, Mr.Iddo."

I was surprised he knew my name. I looked at Mira, and she nodded as well, so I started.

"Thank you, sir. I understand the orders we were given, but in truth, sir, the whole convoy formation is not good enough. It doesn't work against these Silent."

Now he was curious.

"Continue."

"Well, sir. The Silent study us for days undetected, they know exactly what they are targeting when they engage. They have higher range than ever, they are able to be invisible for longer than ever, keep up with our speed, and choose the moment of attack. When they do, they can approach almost undetected before it's too late. They engage very quickly and very deadly. There is no chance whatsoever that the convoy can get into a defensive position in time for it to be effective. Not even for the escorts to get into offensive position! They hit us, they run, and they disappear. Well before anybody can do anything."

Saltz flinched. He looked at Mirany and back at me.

"And you know this how?" he asked. I avoided the question.

"This convoy formation is obsolete, sir. Maintaining relative positions once we're attacked is the wrong thing to do. Ignoring any signal whatsoever from the probes is the wrong thing to do. Trying to circle around once we're attacked is completely ineffective. Relying on wide area weapons to respond is next to useless. If you analyze the data of what happened, you'll find out I'm right. The Silent are much better prepared for the fight. They are way ahead of us."

Saltz sat back, looked at Mirany and asked.

"You agree with your officer?"

She smiled.

"He saved my ship."

Saltz looked back at me.

"So what do you propose, Lieutenant?"

I shrugged.

"I'm not sure, sir."

Saltz turned to his F.O.

"Is Captain Neehan already here?"

Neehan was the *Loghi's* Captain. Apparently, he had also been called and was waiting.

"Yes, sir."

"Well, tell him to come in and join this discussion." The F.O. left, and Saltz looked at us. "You start thinking, then, Mr.Iddo. Start figuring out what to change now, because I don't want to get into a fight with a Silent like this ever again. I'm not sure that disobeying my orders did indeed save you or not, but I'm pretty sure that this could have been much worst. We are sitting ducks. All of us. Every single one of us is meat for the slaughter. We weren't even able to fire one single missile…"

He leaned back in his chair.

"By the way, I don't know if you know already, but it's official."

Mirany and I exchanged glances, then I asked:

"What, sir?"

"War, Mr.Iddo. Axx declared. We're officially at war, now."

I twisted my nose at the irony.

"No kidding…"

*

When we got back to the *Harvy,* a couple of hours later, Mirany presided over the burial of Loly and the other casualties. We launched them into space. It was a sad and short ceremony.

*

We had several discussions with the military over the next few days. It would eventually lead to developments in convoy formation that would be crucial for the rest of the war, as it turned out. But that wouldn't be enough to help QC1.

The Silent came back for us again. And once more. This time the escorts did not ignore the first signals of the probes and acted quickly, not allowing the Silent to come inside the perimeter of the convoy, but still, QC1 lost over 4 million tons of cargo by the time we reached the Eeron and arrived at the space ports of Torrance. The *Harvy,* however, was spared from danger on both occasions. Both attacks came from the starboard bow side, and by the time our ship was able to spot the action the Silent had already disappeared, unharmed, leaving fire and destruction behind.

\*

We got one-week leave after the journey.

Torrance was already under siege. Its ally, the rich planet of Duellot, had been invaded by Axx and it was close enough to serve as a spring board for Axx's bomber ships to reach Torrance. The military bases in Torrance's five moons had been working around the clock to defend against attacks and, amazingly, they had been able to succeed most of the times, repelling even the most massive of attacks.

On the far end of Torrance, there was an area called Uthon that was permanently secure from harm once the Adri moon's orbit would follow the rotation of the planet and be constantly present in the sky. Adri was a fortress, so the Uthon region was a safe haven. And so we were sent there for our leave.

The *Harvy's* crew and officers were accommodated in the town of Athzim. Most of the crew was given quarters in military installations, but the officers stayed at a local hotel. On the first evening, Zhany and Kritia decided to sleep as much as they could, and Rock just sat on the corner of the hotel bar and got very drunk.

Mira and I left to take a walk. There was a local carnival going on, for which the town was famous. In time of war, the carnival attracted even more people from the surrounding areas, trying to forget all that was going on on the other side of the planet.

The weather was hot, and people were loud, chanting and dancing in abandonment. Mira had left her overalls behind and was wearing khaki pants and a casual blue blouse. Her hair was pinned on the top of her head, and a few drops of sweat slid down her long neck. I could hardly take my eyes off her. And she spotted that. It happened in one moment when two boys and one girl passed her by with big fans and saw her sweating and decided to cool her down with frantic joyful moves of the colorful fans. It was surprising, and Mira just started to laugh loud as they sang and waved the fans. And then they left, and Mira looked at me, still laughing, and suddenly realized the way I was looking at her. And it was just a second. A short stare. But it was enough. She came to me, she put her arms around my neck, and she kissed me deeply.

I pulled her to me, but then pushed her off.

"No," I said, under the loud noise of the street. "I'm a Navy officer, you're my Captain, I can't…"

She smiled and said:

"Ok."

And she turned away. But I couldn't let her go. I grabbed her arm before she got lost in the crowd, and pulled her to me and kissed her passionately.

And didn't let go.

Ever.

# INTERLUDE A - TOURISTS

The airship was cruising smoothly over the breathtaking landscapes of Webbur's southern hemisphere. Colors of green, violet and red could be admired from the small windows of the cabins, but Ruzz Schaaks was anxious to leave for breakfast in the panoramic restaurant, where the clean large glass windows would offer a grand view of the lands below. Still, he had to wait. As usual, Mayr Schaaks was taking her time getting ready. Maybe it was the hat, maybe the hair, maybe the dress, something would always demand a lot more time than previously expected.

Ruzz felt uneasy in that first class cabin. He couldn't pinpoint the reason. The cabin was luxurious by any standards, with the small but comfortable living room allowing for an agreeable rest, or an agreeable wait, next to the sleeping room. Still, he felt... watched. How could they be watched? They were many hundreds of palms above ground. The only way to see inside was from below. So why would he feel like that? He looked at the closet. He resisted the urge to look inside the closet. There was nothing there. Nothing but some clothes and accessories a maid had dutifully arranged upon their arrival. And then there was the bar. Small, but well provided. Ruzz knew they made small cameras, nowadays. The size of match boxes. Small enough to be concealed anywhere. Maybe they were watching. He pushed that feeling out of his mind. It wasn't useful. It could jeopardize everything. And then… There was really nothing to watch anyway. They were an average married couple happy to be on this nice sightseeing trip.

Ruzz called to the room.

"Honey, we're missing the whole morning!"

"In a minute!" Replied her voice.

But Ruzz was unable to relax. He went to the bar, picked up a jar of water and served himself. As he drank, he opened the closet's door ever so slightly. Nothing to see. Nothing but the clothes, and the handmade bags neatly stored in the back. He closed the door at the same time as the door to the room opened wide, and Mrs.Schaaks came out with a lovely summer dress made on purpose for her slender figure and a large white hat to match.

"There!" She announced. "I'm almost ready!"

Ruzz frowned.

"Almost?"

She went to the closet, smiling.

"Just relax, darling. We're on vacation. What could be so urgent?"

"The vacation will last only a few weeks, honey. I'm not too keen on spending half the time waiting to go have breakfast."

She opened a drawer and took out a bottle of perfume she used on herself.

"Don't be a bore, darling. The more you wait, the better the taste. I'm aiming to increase your pleasure. That's a wife's role, isn't it?"

Ruzz squeezed his lips and sighed.

"Let's go, then."

"At your command, darling." She said, jumping forth, as lovely as ever. Even though she was only a few years younger than him, she looked fresh as a young girl. How did she do that? As Mayr walked to the door, Ruzz looked around the room.

"Are you content with this room?" He asked.

Mayr raised her eyebrow.

"Very. Why?"

He raised his shoulders.

"Oh, nothing... It's just..." He brushed away that uncomfortable feeling. "Never mind. Let's go."

And they left.

*

About a minute after the Schaaks left the cabin, Nina Zauer came out of the wall. The gel-like white camouflage she had applied to the wall stuck to her whole body. She moved her arms and legs, shaking off the stiffness from several hours of being completely still. Then she was all business. She went directly to the closet. She took out one of the bags. She knew exactly which one. From a small well-concealed pocket under her arm, she took her tools. She used them to open the bag's lock. Then her skilled fingers felt the lining until she found the secret compartment. She used her tools again, and she opened it. There is was. The small black chip. She put it in the small pocket along with her tools.

She was placing the bag back in place when she felt the door of the cabin opening. Moving silently but swiftly, she went into the closet and closed it behind her. She could see very little out, but enough to observe Ruzz Schaaks crossing the room with an annoyed expression on his face. He went into the sleeping room. Nina waited very still. Suddenly, she noticed a very slight footprint of camouflage gel printed on the carpet. From a concealed sheath she took a sharp blade. If Ruzz noticed the footprint she would have to kill him, even though that would jeopardize the whole mission, she would have no choice.

Ruzz came back to the room with a woman's white purse in his hand. He was going out, but he stopped and looked around. Something was off. Nina prepared herself. But finally, Ruzz shrugged and left the cabin. Nina sighed. She stayed put. She would wait a few more minutes before cleaning the room of any signs of her presence and then vanish. She had a cabin of her own, and a solid alias and means at her disposal. She would vanish, and she would never see the Schaaks again.

*

Ruzz Schaaks met with Mayr in the corridor, where she was waiting, looking outside, to the wild and colorful landscape as far as the eyes could see. She took the purse from his hands.

"And?" She asked.

He nodded.

"She was there."

She contained a smile.

"So it's done?"

He nodded again.

"It's done."

She embraced his arm, and they started walking as a loving married couple on vacation would.

"I'll call it in." She said. And then they would have breakfast.

# EPISODE 3 - BACK

Captain Mirany Cavo leaned against her chair on the bridge of the *W.S.Harry*. Her hands rested on her overalls' pockets. Her eyes rested on the dark, non-existent horizon. The convoy was returning to Webbur. We were heading back home.

I feigned an itch and caught a glimpse of Mira's profile. Her lovely straight nose, her calm forehead, smooth eyebrows, flowing blond hair. A flash came to my mind. A flash of her beautiful body, naked, sleeping.

\*

Her beautiful white body sleeping beside me, in the hot, quiet morning. Her round breasts sagging just enough to be even more attractive, her ribs showing a bit, her firm stomach with a drop of sweat sliding forever, her smooth legs…

Mira's eyes opened slightly. She smiled with her perfect mouth. I leaned down. The tip of my nose caressed her inner tight. I knew that smooth part of her body. I knew it well. I had wandered there a few times already. My nose picked up the scent that always took me by suggestive surprise every time it hunted down there for tantalizing treats. I kissed her tight. Her lips were expecting me further on. Already wet. Already waiting. I licked her. Her whole body shook when I did it. Her slender fingers entangled in my hair. She moaned a little. She squirmed. And again. I took my time. A long time. Comfortable between her legs. Anywhere between her legs. Once my loins, once my torso and my hands, now my head and my lips. It didn't matter. I felt comfortable, while she shook, and twisted and squirmed. While she moaned and sighed in the end. I felt at home.

I went up and looked into her eyes. I made a fake salute.

"Captain..." I joked.

She lost her smile.

"Don't." She said, seriously. "Don't."

She was right. It wasn't funny. I kissed her with my lips wet from her juices. She kissed me back. Then she pushed me gently to the side. She crawled down. And she engulfed me with her mouth. There were these little games she played down there. With her lips, and her tongue, and occasionally, with her teasing teeth. She did it for as long as it took. Having fun. In a gift. A very deliberate, obvious and primal gift. Until I came.

Later, we were putting our boots on, back to back, each of us on each side of the bed.

"This can't happen again" I started, my heart stuck in my throat. "I'm a Navy officer. If they find out..."

"It won't." She interrupted. "It won't."

She got up, starting to leave. But I stopped her.

"Wait."

I pushed her to me. We kissed passionately. Then she caressed my cheek, gently. Then she left.

\*

"First buoy up ahead, Captain."

We were entering the Eeron, Zhany was announcing. Mira said nothing. She was worried. I knew she was worried. And I knew why. We had the hulls full of people. Refugees. Thousands of them. Mostly women and children. And after our first few crossings, none of us was deluded about the danger we were in. About the chances we had of surviving again. There was a counter machine somewhere, somehow, trying to figure out the average runs a ship was expected to do before it was destroyed. But it was too soon to tell. Too early in the war to know. We just knew it wouldn't be many.

"Second buoy, 11-11, as expected, Captain."

"Very well" replied Mirany. She got up. We were well under way to cross the Eeron, there wasn't much she could do on the bridge. It would take more than a day for us to clear the asteroid belt. She was nervous, but she forced herself to look calm and composed. She looked at me. It was a casual, professional look. I smiled a little, giving her strength.

"You have the bridge, X.O."

"Yes, Captain, I have the bridge."

*

Even when we were on Webbur, there wasn´t much time to get away from the fleet. More than not, we were posted in the same hotels, waiting or preparing for the next convoy.

I watched her sitting alone at the hotel bar, drinking *awrey* on the rocks. Her blouse a button too open, too careless. Maybe already tipsy. Her blond hair flowing over the shoulders.

"Hi, stranger," I said. "Can I buy you a drink?"

"Sure, stranger." She smiled. "As long as you take me

to bed afterwards."

"Your wish is… well, my wish too." I didn't want to say «command».

She almost laughed.

"You're such a lousy one-liner, Byl. But I'm too drunk to care."

I raised my glass.

"To the *Harvy.*"

"Fuck, yeah." She replied, raising her glass. "May she leave us alone for a few days, so we can fuck like rabbits."

I was probably a little drunk myself, and she was as beautiful as ever.

"Fuck, yeah. That's the best toast I ever heard!"

She emptied her glass, I emptied mine. Then she got up, and looked me in the eye and said:

"Come with me, kiddo. Right now."

I just followed her. We barely made it to the room. She closed the door and assaulted my mouth with hers, and I almost ripped her blouse open and took her breasts in my hands, and then in my mouth. She made me trip down to the floor, and she grabbed my penis hard through the pants, I almost screamed in pain and took the trousers off as fast as I could, at the same time she took hers off, and we were naked, and she jumped me and mounted me, and we fucked hard, and then I rolled over her, and pinned her hands to the floor and got deep inside her, as far and as fast as I could. And then we moaned hard, together, like animals. Feeling like animals. Loving it. Loving each other's animal. Wild. Bursting through every inch of skin.

Then it was over, and we stayed there. I looked into her eyes, her watery blue eyes, and she looked into mine, our breaths very close to each others'. And she said:

"Stay inside me."

"I will," I said.

"As long as you can."

"I will," I said. I rolled back, so she came on top, again,

and let her rest her head on my chest, and she slept. Peacefully.

\*

"X.O."

I looked at Zhany.

"What is it?"

"Priority call, sir. For you and the Captain. From Captain Saltz."

This convoy was the HC14. Saltz was leading the run again. That was the third time we had him. And the truth was: we were getting to like him more and more. The conversations we had, on QC1 and after that, had led to more conversations higher up the chain of command, and the formation of the convoys had changed very quickly.

The 20-ship long parallel lines traveling fast through empty space was a thing of the past. Now we moved in a compact square. 7 ships by 7. At least an escort on each side of the square, so it would take them a lot less time to get next to any one ship in the formation. This meant the whole convoy had to travel slower. And each ship had to be careful not to get off the path in the slightest, or she could bump into another. There had been discussions of making the convoys into cubes, even tighter. But a simple square gave it more flexibility for there could always be escape routes up or down. As far as we were concerned, this formation was far better than the parallel lines. And it had been impressive how quickly it had evolved.

"Inform the Captain, then."

"Yes, sir."

We had five escorts, on this trip. Two at the rear (one a little bit up, another a little bit down), and the other three on each side. The *Ascim* was on point, as usual. And we had the *Loghi* on our left flank again.

"Sir, the *Ayari* reports an asteroid on the starboard

side," said Rock, at the helm. "The convoy is shifting two degrees port."

"You can change your course, Rock."

"Aye, sir, changing course."

No one called anyone 'sir,' on the *Harvy*. But they got used to calling me 'sir.' Don't know why.

"The Captain asks you to join her in her quarters for the call, sir." Said Zhany.

I raised my eyebrow. That was unusual.

"Very well" I replied. "The bridge is yours, Rock."

"Yes, sir."

*

There was a secret pact between us. A pact that said that while aboard, we didn't touch each other, we didn't kiss, we didn't show any sign of affection. This was our ship. Our baby. And we would take care of it as we were supposed to. Professionally. A complicit smile was all we actually shared once in a while, to remind us of what we were to each other. It was strange, overall, but it was what we did. Our ritual. Our way.

Captain Saltz's call was passed through to Mira's office. I sat next to her, and we both hailed the Navy officer.

"Mr.Iddo, I'm going to need you, I'm afraid."

"Sir?"

"We had an incident aboard the *Loghi*. A couple, actually."

"Anything serious, sir?"

"Well, you could say that. Captain Neehan had an accident. Fell down a flight of stairs on a drill and bumped his head. He won't be fit for action for a while. He was actually evacuated to the *Ascim*, we have a better medical ward."

"Is he okay?" asked Mirany.

"He will be in a few days. Meanwhile, his second in command took over the ship, but he ran into a bit of trouble."

"A bit of trouble, sir?" I raised my eyebrow.

"This was his first command, and it seems he is not prepared for it. Or something. We may have misjudged the boy."

"Something happened?" inquired Mira.

"You could say that. It took him 24 hours to get a mutiny on his hands."

"A mutiny? What do you mean?"

"It seems the men simply stopped following his orders, I'm not sure. We will have an inquiry. But the boy closed himself in his cabin for a day, and we ended up having to bring him up to the *Ascim* as well. The second lieutenant has assumed command, but I would much rather have someone a bit more senior running that frigate. She's 20% of our firepower. She must be in top condition. I was wondering if we could count on Mr.Iddo for the job, Captain."

An avalanche of feelings burst inside my mind. What the hell! Back to the Navy? The proper Navy? At the command of a frigate!? This... this was an old dream coming true! However... Leaving the *Harvy*... Leaving Mira.... I couldn't. But was it real? Commanding a frigate? A convoy escort? What the hell!?

I looked at Mira, hesitant, not knowing what to do. I wouldn't leave her, but... Her face was calm, confident. She knew what to do.

"Of course, Captain," she said. "When do you need him?"

I was shocked. The easiness with which she said that. So calm. Was she indifferent to my presence? Didn't she care?

"Well... As soon as possible, I would say" replied Saltz.

"He'll be ready presently," she said.

"Oh, good."

"I'll send a shuttle to the *Loghi* in… what do you say, Mr.Iddo, an hour?"

I felt paralyzed. I didn't know what to do. I was divided. I couldn't answer her question. I felt as if my heart and my brain were bumping hard against each other. All had been decided as if I wasn't even there.

"Would that be enough, lieutenant?" she asked again.

I looked at her, mesmerized. She was so calm. So composed. I… I didn't know what to think. She finally looked back to Captain Saltz and answered for me.

"Mr.Iddo is just coming out of a long shift, Captain, and he is a bit tired. But I'm sure he will be able to take command of the *Loghi* before he rests, isn't that so, Mr. Iddo?"

"Y… Yes" I managed.

"He'll leave before the hour, Captain Saltz," she said.

"That's perfect!" smiled Saltz. "I need that ship in good hands. Don't let me down. Over and out."

Saltz's face disappeared from the screen. I looked at Mira. She looked at me. And inside a second her face let slip three revealing expressions: pride in me, then worry, then… fear. Like she thought she'd never see me again. Like she didn't want to lose me. And then her face just went calm and smooth again. And I felt like I'd learned more about her in that second than in the last month.

"I can't leave." My voice faltered.

"You must." She murmured.

"The *Harvy* is my ship. You are my Captain." I felt childish, I felt foolish, but I couldn't stop myself. For the past few months, I'd seen her every day. We worked as a team. We were one. We cared for our baby. And now I was going to leave for weeks. Far away. As if in different planets.

"You're Navy. We're at war. You'll protect us better

from the _Loghi_." Her voice trembled. "You must."

She was telling the truth. It was my duty. I had to go. And that was that. All else was completely irrelevant. And yes, I would be able to better protect our baby from the frigate. And if that was so, there was no other place I should be. It was my duty. My duty as an officer, my duty as an X.O, my duty as a partner, and my duty as a father.

I stood up.

"I'll get my gear ready."

I turned to leave, but she caught my arm, pulled me gently to her, put her hands on my neck and kissed me.

"I will always be here," she whispered.

I looked at her with a cold, hard face.

"Don't you dare get killed."

That surprised her. It surprised us both, actually. Hesitant, she stepped back. She saluted me, with a serious gesture, maybe for the first time. I responded with the most perfect salute I ever did. And then I turned and left.

*

"Welcome aboard, sir."

I put my cap on and responded to the lieutenant's salute.

"Mr.Doorbos?"

The young lieutenant smiled. He was young. Maybe 18 or 19.

"Yes, sir."

I put forward my hand.

"Byllard Iddo."

The young man hesitated and then smiled and shook my hand.

"I know, sir. We've been expecting you."

He'd been in charge of the _Loghi_ for the last few hours. I didn't know if his nervous stare was a sign of relieve because I was taking over or some kind of evaluation, trying to figure out if I was up to the job. Maybe a bit of both.

"I don't know if you'd rather meet the officers now, sir," he said. "Or maybe go to your cabin and rest a bit, sir, they tell me…"

"Well, let's meet the officers, why don't we?" I replied.

"Of course, sir. Please follow me."

\*

The *W.S. Loghi* was a 5th class 6-Hull 32-battery frigate with a crew of 2000 men and women. 250 for each hull, 300 in the tower and 200 Marines.

Frigates were a dream to command. They were fast and flexible, usually avoiding the line battles fought by the great battleships that made up the core of the fleets. Yet, they were more powerful than almost any other vessel out there except line ships and destroyers, the prime escorts of anything from battleships to merchants. Frigates were mostly used for long haul patrols, search and destroy, pirate hunt or special missions. But they were useful for everything. They could work as runners and explorers for fleets, escorts for convoys or sharp shooters for flotillas, but they did their best as lone rangers going further and faster than anyone else. Any officer in his right mind would love to command a frigate. And now this one was mine.

It was also a pleasure to be back aboard a Navy ship. Evidence was everywhere, in the efficient way everything was packed and ready, in the spotless way everything was clean and neat, in the impeccable salutes from every hand, in the way everything looked and worked smoothly and effectively. There were no signs of disorder or mutiny anywhere.

\*

The senior officers were waiting for me in the

Captain's office. The C-Team, five of them, plus six Hull-Captains, plus the Marine Major, plus the master-of-the-tower. They all lined up to salute me, and Doorbos introduced me to all. Most of them were young, even though there were three or four that had been in the service for many years, possibly passed for promotion and, who knows? resentful of cocky young officers like me. Which of them had encouraged the revolt?

I suddenly felt really tired, I had been on duty for over 14 hours, and I was dying to lie down, so I said:

"I'm sure we'll have a chance to know each other better in the coming days. Right now I'd like to ask you just one question."

They all looked nervous and uncomfortable, maybe fearing I'd ask about the mutiny or any disturbance in the ship. But I asked:

"Is the ship ready for action? In all honesty, and I remind you that our lives and others' may depend on it: is she ready for action?"

They tighten their bellies, straighten their backs and answered one after the other.

"Yes, sir."

"Absolutely, sir."

"Certainly!"

And they were serious. There wasn't any doubt in any voice. They were confident of their performance.

"Good, then. That's enough for now. Carry on."

Before everyone left, I called Steld, the Signals Commander and asked to be called if 'any strange contact whatsoever was picked up anywhere.' Finally, everyone was gone except for Doorbos, and I told him:

"Now, please take me to my cabin, Mr.Doorbos. I think I'll have some rest, now."

As I laid my head down a few minutes later, I recalled my entrance into this crew's life finding it had been rough and clumsy. I hadn't been able to say anything clever nor really pay attention to any of the officers. I wondered if they'd hate me already. Much later I would learn that I actually had impressed them all. Go figure.

*

One time, we had a two weeks' vacation in Webbur. We'd just run three high-risk convoys back-to-back, and we were exhausted. The last one, HC8, had been attacked five times along the way. It was just luck that kept us going.

Mira had wanted to take me to a cabin in the woods near a lake she knew, up in the Hobaka ridge, in Obata. We took the train. As soon as the train was under way, Mira told me:

"I'm going to the bathroom."

"I'm going with you," I replied.

We closed the door, we jumped into each other, almost ripping all our clothes off. She turned around and put her hands firmly on the mirror, I yanked down her panties and entered her from behind. Frantic. We both were. Frantic. We had to fight to contain our screams. When we got back to our seats, she fell asleep on my shoulder.

Curiously enough, sex got milder after that. That was the trip that changed some things. That changed everything. Sex lost priority on that trip, and other things took its place. Better things, even. Like holding hands by the lake, swimming naked side by side, sailing in the morning, kissing in the moonlight, dancing slowly on the porch, waking up side by side, cooking for each other. At one point, looking at her sitting on the couch reading poetry, I thought those had been the best days I ever had.

But then we had to come back. There was a war on.

*

"Sit down, Lieutenant."

Doorbos sat across my desk. The Captain's desk. Rested and clean-shaved, I suddenly felt confident there. Like it was second-nature. But I had some questions still.

"I'm not here to look into the mutiny, nor anything else that happened before I came aboard." I started. "But I need to know. I need to know the ship is fully functional. I can't see any sign of disorder or ill-will. So, what happened here?"

"Well, sir, I don't think you'll find anything wrong right now. Captain Neehan run a tight ship."

"Mutinies don't happen in tight ships, Mr.Doorbos."

"Well... There was cause."

"What happened, Mr.Doorbos?"

"Well, sir, when Captain Neehan had the accident, Mr.Voica assumed command. He was never a much-respected officer, sir. He was here because of family ties and never really earned affection from anyone."

"To the point, please, Mr.Doorbos." I wasn't about letting any man openly criticize an officer like that – even a disgraced one.

"Well, sir. Practically his first order of business, other than transferring the Captain, was ordering an FQ drill. You see, this is our third convoy in a row, sir, without rest, and we'd just had a drill that ended up in the Captain's accident."

A Full Quarters drill, or FQ drill, was a full ship battle stations drill that included some exhausting exercises as fully loading the missile batteries over and over again. I could understand that taking such a drill after losing the commanding officer like that could have been extremely unpopular, and instead of asserting command, work the other way around.

"So, what happened, sir" continued Doorbos "is that on the first time 5th Hull wasn't pitch perfect, so Mr.Voica ordered us to drill once more. But 1st Hull refused, sir, and then 2nd Hull refused as well. You see, the men were exhausted, sir. And when Mr.Voica called the Marine MP's to take the officers to the brig, Major Glavin refused to do it as well, sir. Pretty soon everyone refused his orders, and he locked himself in his cabin and didn't come out until the officers from the *Ascim* came to take him. And that was that. I know that mutiny is severely punished, sir."

"By death, Mr.Doorbos."

"Yes, sir. But you've seen the ship, you've met the officers. They're good officers, sir. Very unlike Mr.Voica, sir. He had no business commanding this ship, sir, or any other, if you ask me."

"I'm not. I'm not asking you, Mr.Doorbos."

I didn't like what Doorbos was saying, and I had to let him know. Voica might have been an incompetent idiot, but I was far from condoning a mutiny of any kind.

"It's the Navy's job to decide who commands a ship, lieutenant, not the men's."

"Yes, sir. Of course, sir."

"I'm not here to assert blame for the situation; that will be done by others once we arrive in Webbur. But I will have no insubordination from anyone, and that has to be made perfectly clear. Do you understand, Mr.Doorbos?"

"Yes, sir. Of course, sir. Perfectly clear."

But it wasn't clear. He still asked:

"Would you want to do something about that, sir?"

"Do?"

"I don't know… A gesture, sir. To make it clear?"

I didn't understand the suggestion. Was the discipline so affected that it needed a gesture to assert it above the words of the Captain to his second in command? I asked:

"A gesture? A disciplinary gesture? Would you recommend that, Mr.Doorbos?"

"I wouldn't, sir."

"Good, then. That will do."

"Yes, sir. Thank you, sir."

His face filled with relief and he saluted me and left. I found out later that Captain Neehan was fond of some manipulative gestures, and then understood that Voica's drill was a page out of that manual as well. Fortunately, I had other schooling. In ships much larger, more important and better run.

*

I made my best to know the ship as quickly and as deeply as I could. In two days, I visited every Hull, conferred with every captain, inspected the tower top to bottom. By the second day in, every single hand in the ship had seen my face. I was mostly pleased with what I saw. But I hadn't seen them in action yet.

*

The master-of-the-tower was a sullen man of 50, with a thin nose and a cold stare. His name was Tamburo, Patt Tamburo. Unlike most people, to whom he was rude and blunt, it took me 30 seconds to start to like him.

"How well is the tower, Mr. Tamburo?"

"Tight."

"Really tight?"

"No. But tight enough, Captain. Most of the lads don't need the whip most of the time. The occasional smarty. No idiots."

He wasn't speaking of a real whip, of course. That was a thing of the past. But I knew what he meant.

"Fast to call?" I asked.

"Fast enough."

I raised my eyebrow.

"Fast enough for the Silent?"

"Barely, sir. But they'll do if you give 'em a chance."

I smiled.

"It's not me who's going to give them a chance, Mr. Tamburo. It's the enemy."

"Aye, sir. That he will."

"Advise?"

"Some meat, sir."

"Meat?"

"There's not a lot of energy around, right now, they're a bit tired. And I reckon they will need some energy if they have that chance you just mentioned, sir."

I thought for a couple of seconds.

"Very well, master-of-the-tower. Meat it is. Please tell the cook. But remind everyone I will be expecting that energy."

"Yes, sir."

*

The bridge of the *Loghi*. I hadn't been on a frigate in a long time, and the bridge of the *Loghi* looked like the most beautiful place I'd ever seen. Smaller than the large bridge of a first-tier battleship, it could accommodate 7 to 9 people. That made it cozier and more controllable. Otherwise, it looked pretty much as a battleship bridge. It had a mimicking display all around, showing the space around the ship and making us feel as if suspended in Space. It had a Captain's chair above the one of the First Officer. And the various consoles could be turned to any direction. Everything a Navy ship-of-war should have. It didn't have a Constellation display, showing in 3D the relative position of everyone in the fleet or convoy, but that didn't dent in the least the extraordinary feeling I had as I entered the room.

"Captain on deck! Attention!" Shouted Doorbos, behind me, as we got in.

Everyone got up quickly into attention. That felt good. That felt really good.

"That will do," I said.

Steld, the S-Comm, was running the bridge at that point. He saluted me and asked:

"Will you assume, sir?"

"No need, thank you, Mr.Steld. The bridge is yours, carry on."

"Yes, sir."

He sat down on the F.O. chair, leaving the Captain's to me, as dictated protocol. I asked Doorbos to introduce me to everyone, and after I had shaken everyone's hand, I sat on that high chair. It felt good. I sat quietly.

Doorbos, standing next to me, tried to engage me in conversation twice, but finally, I dismissed him.

"You can go, Mr.Doorbos. I'm sure you're needed elsewhere. I'll call you when necessary."

He was a bit surprised but saluted me and left.

I sat quietly in the bridge for about an hour. After the first 20 minutes, everyone almost forgot I was there. In that hour, I felt as I was becoming part of the ship and the ship was becoming part of me. The crew got comfortable as well. Comfortable with my presence. And that felt right.

Finally, I got up with a smile and said:

"Thank you, Mr.Steld. Carry on."

And I left. It had been a mystical experience.

*

That night I called Mirany. It was so good to see her face. To hear her voice. Only then did I realize how tired I was. I was finally relaxing a bit.

"How's your new ship?" She asked.

"Interesting. Clean and tidy."

She could hear the pride in my voice.

"Tight?" She asked.

"Tight enough."

She gave me a sad smile.

"Good to be back in the Navy, then?"

I gave her back a sad smile, not knowing what to say. It was, and it wasn't.

"It is, and it isn't. How's the *Harvy?*"

She gave me another smile. Different. Like she was looking at a family picture.

"Oh, fine! Chaotic!"

"What do you mean?"

"Well, you know what today is?"

"Today?"

"It's the Day of the Jewel! And we seem to have about a thousand children on board, so they have been doing the rounds, complimenting everybody and distributing whatever candy they found who knows where. I had the cooks bake cakes in every hull!"

I laughed, imagining the refugee children around anyone I remembered. That sounded lovely. Her face was lovely.

"I wish I was there." And, for a moment, I meant it.

"Me too. I don't know if we can manage it on our own. The Silent we can handle. But these little boys and girls... The Axx Republic messed with the wrong people, let me tell you. I may have to retire, after this."

And I laughed again.

"You're loving it," I said.

She smiled back, tenderly.

"Who wouldn't?"

That was my Mira.

\*

It was two days later that I was called in the middle of my sleep.

"Captain, sir." It was Mass, my 16-year-old orderly, shaking me gently by the arm. "Sorry to disturb you, sir."

"What is it, Mr.Mass?"

"You asked to be called if there was a contact."

I jumped from my bed and looked at him straight in the eye.

"Get my shirt."

I put on my trousers like a lover hearing the husband coming in. As Mass handed me the shirt, he immediately picked up the boots as well. In less than two minutes I was out of the door.

I calmed down before entering the bridge. I didn't step in as if strolling around, like Mirany would do. I entered like Admiral Hedde did: quiet, affirmative, straight to his chair.

"I have the bridge."

"The Captain has the bridge." Said Doorbos, leaving my chair and taking his own.

I looked at my screens and glanced at the Signals screen, but then I remembered: I was the Captain.

"Mr.Steld, please put the flag on the MID."

"Sir!"

Doorbos filled me in:

"Contact at Level 12, 10-and-11, sir. Could be nothing."

I looked at him and knew that even he didn't believe that. There had been enough convoys, victims, and defeats, to have learned no contact was 'nothing.' I spoke directly to him, for there was no special Captain-First Officer communication line, as Hedde had on the *Magnar*.

"This was 10 minutes ago?"

"Yes, sir."

"Hmm. Did you relay it to the *Ascim?*"

"Yes, sir. As ordered."

"Good. Clear the boards, then, please, Mr.Doorbos."

"Yes, sir! Clearing the boards."

We were too far from the asteroid belts for it to be nothing. It was too rare the occasions that we found a rock stranded in the middle of nowhere. Statistically insignificant occasions. If it wasn't a glitch, it was something. And every single contact with a Silent started this way. Yet, 10 minutes was a long time. We should have had another contact at this point. Anything.

"Probes, Mr.Steld?"

"338 minutes, sir."

Probe technology had improved very quickly. Probes lasted longer, nowadays.

"Good."

We waited another 10 minutes. Nothing. The bridge was completely quiet.

"A glitch, sir?" asked Doorbos.

"No. She's out there, lieutenant."

I looked around. Dark space all around. Where was she?

"Enhanced positions, please, Mr.Steld."

"Sir."

He pushed the button and circles of yellow light appeared on the MID and showed the positions of the other ships in the convoy, on the starboard side, where they were supposed to be. The port side, to the left, was just dark and empty. She could be anywhere. But she was out there. If we did nothing, I knew what would happen. She would be inside the convoy before we knew it. Creating mayhem. We waited 10 more minutes before I decided.

"Well, this is enough." I sat back in the chair. "Mr.Valero."

Valero was the N-Comm.

"Sir?"

"One-degree starboard, if you please, and minus 5% velocity."

"Sir?"

Everyone was looking at me. They couldn't quite believe the order. I was leaving my position in the convoy. It was badly accepted when a merchant ship did this, but for an escort Navy vessel to leave position… I was doing it again… But my eyes fell over Valero like a rock.

"You heard me, Mr.Valero. One degree starboard, minus 5% velocity. Now."

Valero swallowed hard, opened his eyes wide and immediately jumped to his console.

"Yes, sir!"

The *Loghi* started to move slowly to the right, getting closer to the convoy. A murmur of astonishment ran through the bridge. I wished I had F.O. Orrey there to shut it up. But Doorbos was as surprised and frozen as the rest of them. He looked at me, timid.

"Is this wise, sir?" He managed the courage to whisper to me.

I smiled, trying to show confidence.

"She was at Level 12, 30 minutes ago. Where do you think she might be now?"

He thought a little before answering.

"Probably getting in position, sir. Probably going for the butt."

I smiled again. He was clever, after all.

"Then we need to get in a better position ourselves, don't we?"

He thought again.

"Yes, sir. I guess we do. But, sir... Our orders..."

"CONTACT! Level 7, 8-and-9, sir!"

Leveled and back. Those were the Silent I knew. They went back and leveled. The whole bridge looked at me, in expectation. You could hear a pin drop...

"Mr.Valero."

He came out of the trance, almost surprised.

"Sir?"

"Cut velocity by 40%."

"Sir?"

I gave him the cold stare again.

"That's the last time you question my orders, Mr.Valero. Minus 40 velocity, on the double!"

"Yes, SIR!"

"Gentlemen," I said. "This is it. I'm counting on you. Webbur is counting on you. Let's do what we're here to do."

There was a bit of whispering again. Doorbos looked at me. There was a new determination in his eyes. A smile of madness also. Something different. Was it me who had that effect on him?

"Battle stations, Captain?" he asked.

I smiled back.

"Battle stations, First Officer."

Battle stations were called. Our velocity decreased, we were drifting fast towards the back of the convoy. The bridge was frantic at that point. I looked to see if everyone had their seat belts on, but this was Navy, not a merchant ship, and of course, they had them on.

"I need Weapons ready, Mr.Kreen!" I groaned.

"Yes, sir! Almost there!"

"Now, Mr.Kreen!"

"Yes, sir! "

Kreen started pressing all the hulls to get ready. I could see that the frigate, still moving a degree starboard, was dangerously approaching a merchant, and Valero had twisted his chair straight towards the stern and was getting nervous. I knew this had to be right, it was going to be close, but we needed the position. Valero looked at me.

"Captain…"

"Steady as she goes, lieutenant, steady as she goes."

"SIR!" shouted Steld. "Captain Saltz is hailing, sir. Inquiring about our movements."

"Tell him we're engaging, lieutenant." I turned my chair towards the back. We were approaching the *Slingard,* a 700k-ton merchant, very rapidly. I tapped Doorbos violently on the shoulder. "Weapons!"

"WEAPONS, MR.KREEN!" Shouted Doorbos.

"Oh, the stars!" Someone said.

"The *Slingard* is signaling, sir! COLLISION

WARNING!!"

The *Slingard* started turning starboard, trying to escape.

"Oh, BY THE STARS!" Said the same someone.

"WE'RE GONNA HIT, CAPTAIN!!" Shouted Valero.

"NOW, MR.VALERO, CORRECT 2 DEGREES! NOW!"

Valero obeyed as quickly as only a Webbur Navy specialist could and our bow turned left at the same time we saw the *Slingard* passing next to us at no more than 500 palms on the starboard side.

"Gods and angels…" Someone said.

"MR.KREEN!!" I shouted.

"WEAPONS READY, SIR!!"

"CONTACT!! LEVEL 0!! 6-AND-9!!"

I looked up. At level zero there was no hiding, the mimic display showed the Silent dark boat right behind us!

"Fuck! She's on top of us!" Said Doorbos.

"COLLISION, CAPTAIN!!" Shouted Valero.

"STEADY!" I ordered.

"Oh, The Stars!!"

"TORPEDOES!!!" Shouted Steld.

We actually saw the black torpedoes coming out of the slick vessel, coming at us with a dark gray tail of smoke behind them.

"Oh, shit!"

"Oh, gods!"

"FUCK!!!"

But the torpedoes, still unarmed, passed by us, one on each side. I think I even saw the white markings on their flanks! And then the devices fired their engines and sped up towards the *Slingard*. But we were all looking back, at the Silent boat coming towards us, climbing desperately.

"COLLISION!!" Shouted Valero.

"STEADY!" I ordered again.

And the Silent accelerated upwards, and we cleared it

from the bottom. We actually saw the whole dark hull passing over our heads, at arm's length.

"Oh, Gods!"

"Mr.Valero, full speed ahead, 40-degrees port, 10-degrees down and roll!" I ordered. "Give her the flank!"

And he acted without delay. Knew exactly what to do. The *Loghi* turned left and leaned. The Silent understood what we were doing and started turning starboard, away from us. But it was too late.

"Fire at will, Mr.Kreen!"

"SIR! ALL EVEN READY! FIRE!"

Our starboard broadside was aiming right at the enemy. We could see the red hot of their burners. We could see the tower and the dark hull. 160 missiles roared from their batteries, and for a moment we saw nothing else but the white smoke from their engines.

"THE ENEMY IS FIRING, SIR!"

"Countermeasures."

"COUNTERMEASURES, YES SIR!"

But we were too close. Countermeasures had no hope. We would be hit. But we weren't a merchant, we were a frigate. And frigates endure.

"Hold on," I said, suddenly feeling calm.

"OH, GODS!!!"

And we got hit. Several missiles hit us on the starboard side. It felt like we were in a violent earthquake. Everything shook! Smoke came out of a pipe in a wall, in the middle of the display, until someone closed a valve.

"The enemy, Mr.Steld!" I asked. "What happened to the enemy!?"

But in a moment, we all could see it: the Silent was exploding all around. We had hit her hard. She wouldn't survive. In a close missile fight, she was out of her league.

"WE GOT HER!" shouted Steld. "WE GOT HER, SIR!"

And then the Silent exploded whole, and all the crew

shouted in joy and laughed out loud. We had her! And there weren't many ships, so far, that could boast bringing down a Silent. I looked up to my right, for a moment, and could see the intact yellow circle out there, where the *Harvy* was. I had protected her. She was safe.

"Mr.Doorbos."

"Sir?" Doorbos looked at me with a big smile on his face.

"Damages, if you please."

"Yes, sir."

Doorbos focused on his console. I looked around confirming everyone was all right.

"Good work, men. Mr.Valero, back to our position, if you don't mind."

"Yes, sir!"

They were still laughing and tapping each other's backs.

"What of the *Slingard*, Mr.Steld?"

"Badly hit, Captain. Two torpedoes. But hanging in."

Many people would have died. I thought back, wondering if there was something else I could have done. Then Doorbos got back to me.

"Sir. We have damages in Hulls 2 and 6, but they're being handled. No active fires. H4 is the worst, sir. They have major breaches back there."

"Red lights?"

"Several, sir."

This was bad. I twisted my nose, uncomfortable.

"Let's close it down."

"Yes, sir."

I picked up the internal communicator and called the Captain of Hull 4. I was surprised I remembered his name, and so was he.

"Captain Sachett, how are things back there?"

"Not that great, sir." His voice was composed, but I could hear screaming in the background. Sachett was a good man, 45,and a sailor to the bone. I had the feeling that if there was someone that could handle it, it was him.

"Casualties?"

"A few, sir, but still don't know how many."

"Do you have gravity?"

"Irregular, sir."

"O2?"

"Managing so far. But 30% of the Hull is off the grid, sir."

"Any fires?"

"A couple, sir. It's going to take a while."

"I'm afraid we're going to have to close you down, Captain." I felt the bile in my mouth as I was saying it.

"Yes, sir."

"We can give you water, power, and oxygen, but that will be it."

"I understand, sir."

"Good luck to you all."

"Thank you, sir. We'll do our best."

"I know you will."

I laid down the mike and looked at Doorbos.

"Close H4."

"Closing H4, yes, sir."

"CONTACT!! LEVEL 8, 10-AND-11!!"

What the fuck?!... What the hell was this? Two Silent Boats in one attack? As far as I knew, that had never happened! The bridge got quiet in an instant. The hesitation was such that Steld decided to repeat the contact info.

"Sir? Cont…"

"Put it on the MID, please, Mr.Steld."

There it was. Another signature. Only a blip, but we all knew what it was. And a sudden chill came up my back. If the Silent was attacking the convoy directly from the left, as she seemed to be, the fact that the *Loghi* had forsaken her position had left the enemy's path wide open.

"Mr.Valero, full speed ahead, for all she's worth! We

need to get back to our position now!"

"Yes, sir! Full speed!"

No one was cheerful anymore. Everyone got focused on their tasks. I looked at the merchant ships ahead. The *Acia*, the *Herret*, the *Zelden* and the *Ezue* were the most exposed. Had I just sacrificed them? And we were coming up close to the *Slingard* once more. The merchant was badly hurt on both sides, discharging heavy debris backwards. Towards us. Valero started turning to avoid it.

"Maintain course, Mr.Valero. Full speed."

"But, sir, the debris…"

"Go through it, lieutenant! We have no time to spare!"

"Yes, sir."

I looked at Doorbos, to see if he had any objections as well, but he was facing the bow smiling madly. Debris started to hit us. Black lumps of metal, just surging from nothing and bumping into the frigate.

"Gods!" shouted someone.

"Gods and angels!" said another.

That was enough.

"THE NEXT PERSON WHO GETS RELIGIOUS ON THIS BRIDGE WILL GET THE BRIG, FOR MY HONOR!" I shouted.

They quieted down. In the next second, a big chunk of debris came up from nowhere and bumped violently on top of us. The whole ship shook.

"Mr.Doorbos?"

"It's the tower, Captain. I think we might have lost it."

That seemed an exaggerated assessment, but I didn't get into it at that point. I turned to Quippel, the Tech-Comm.

"Mr.Quippel, please send somebody up there to confirm it."

"Yes, sir!"

"Contact, sir! Level 5, 10-and-10."

The bitch was doing exactly what I had predicted: she

was heading directly to the vulnerable port side of the convoy. Exactly where we should have been to prevent it.

"Sir!" called Valero. "Should I deviate?"

We were heading directly towards the *Slingard's* thrusters.

"Slightly, Mr.Valero. Starboard side, please." If we went through the left, we would miss our trajectory.

We were still taking bumps from the merchant's debris, but less and less and smaller and smaller. We passed very close to the *Slingard's* starboard side, managing to see the horror going on down there. At least four or even five hulls had been breached on this flank. Many bodies, probably refugees, could still be seen attached to chairs, but there were also holes where others would probably have been. It was a disaster. It was unlikely she would be able to keep up with the convoy until Webbur. But if she made it to the Mirox she would be safe. More or less.

"Sir, it's confirmed," said Quippel at that time. "We lost most of the tower."

Dammit! We had lost good people. And probably much of the C-Team's belongings as well. Because we didn't deviate from the debris. Because I was impetuous! But it had been worth it. I looked at my watch, confirming the time, and then again at my screen. We passed the *Slingard* and finally had open space ahead. And if I had predicted the enemy's route correctly, we might be able to reach her before she could fire her torpedoes. There was a surge of mad elation inside of me. Something crazy, megalomania of some sort. But then...

"SIR! The *Nyban* is reporting contact!! Level 6, 4-and-5!"

What?? Another one? And... I choked. My heart stopped, and suddenly I couldn't breathe. 4-and-5 meant starboard, back and low. Right next to the *Harvy*.

"Please confirm, Mr.Steld."

"Confirmed, sir. Contact, level 6, 4-and-5."

NO, NO, NO, NO, NO, NO, NO! NOT AGAIN! NOT AGAIN! NOT AGAIN! I brought the flag to my console. The screen showed it. It was true. The *Nyban* had called it. The *Nyban*, an old decaying Corvette, run by an adolescent green Captain. The *Harvy* was in danger! In serious danger!

"Weapons, Captain?"

It was Doorbos. He was looking at me.

"What?"

"Is everything all right, Captain?" he whispered. I couldn't take my eyes off my screen, off the image of the *Harvy* on my screen.

"I… I can't…"

"There's nothing you can do, sir." He said, in a low voice, to keep it from others. "She's too far away. Let the *Nyban* have her, sir. We need you here."

I looked into his eyes. His determined eyes. I knew he was right. I had to trust fate. Cruel, wretched fate. I had to trust Mira. She would do all there was to be done. I had to do the same for this ship. For the *Loghi,* my command, my men. I looked up.

"I… Do we…? Do we have 'scatter bombs'?"

I meant MSS1 missiles, which would target a large area. Doorbos nodded.

"Yes, sir."

"The next contact Steld gives you, fire them at that position."

"Yes, sir. Do you think?…"

"No, it won't get her, but do it anyway."

"Yes, sir."

I could trust Doorbos. I could trust Doorbos, for a minute. I needed to calm down. Calm down! Focus! Focus on the *Loghi*. Focus on our foe! *Do your job!*

Doorbos spoke loud.

"Mr.Kreen, I need a 'scatter' sequence ready, odd side!"

"Sir, yes, SIR!"

She would be fine. The *Harvy* would be fine. Luck would hold. She would hold. Mira... Oh, Mira...

"Weapons ready, sir!" That was Kreen.

"Fine, Mr.Kreen. Wait for it!" That was Doorbos.

"Contact, sir! Level 3, 10-and-9!" That was Steld.

"Fire, Mr.Kreen!"

"Hull 1, FIRE! Hull 3, FIRE! Hull 5, FIRE!"

The missiles flew away in succession. We saw them disappearing rapidly into the void until we didn't see them anymore. I looked up and noticed the *Acia* coming up ahead. I almost jumped in my seat.

"Port, Mr.Valero, port!" I called. "We need to get a better position fast!"

"Yes, sir!"

We changed course, to pass the *Acia* by her larboard side. The 'scatter bombs' started blowing up in the dark space, over an incredibly large area, but it was clear that they didn't hit the enemy.

"Good!" I said. "The enemy is between the 'scatter' explosion and the convoy. That's not a lot of space. Get me a 'flash probe' sequence, Mr.Kreen. From 3-10-9 to 1-12-9, on the double!"

"Sir, yes, SIR!"

I meant the PTL30's, the probes that flashed once, burning immediately, but giving us a clear picture of the area. We felt the smooth sound and vibrations of the probes sliding out of their nests and jumping into space. I looked again to my screen. Oh, no!! OH, NO! OH, NO! OH, NO! The *Harvy*! The *Harvy* was being hit! Once and again! The *Harvy* was being hit! I saw explosions, and more! She was being hit! She was being hit! She was lost!

\*

That night, before going to bed, we had talked and

laughed. We were smiling and looking at each other through the screens in each of our cabins. Then I said:

"I love you."

She smiled even more. With her bright green eyes.

"Yes?"

"Yes," I confirmed.

"You know what?" She asked.

"What?" I asked.

"I love you too."

And we stood there, looking at each other like smiling idiots for a few moments. But then there was a veil of sadness between us and she said:

"See you tomorrow."

And I said:

"See you tomorrow."

And off we went.

*

"CONTACT!! Level 2, 11-and-9!! RED FLAG, SIR!"

The probes had flashed. Flashed and showed the enemy. The Silent was right in front of us. Preparing to fire on the merchants. But I couldn't move! I couldn't think! Doorbos got it. He understood. And he knew what to do! He gave the orders immediately:

"70-degrees starboard, Mr.Valero!! Full speed! Give her flank! Mr.Kreen! Fire when ready!! Go get her!"

The *Loghi* violently turned right until she had firing solutions, and Kreen shouted:

"ALL ODDS FIRE!"

And then the ship trembled as the 160 missiles left her side as straight arrows flowing to the target. Then, Steld shouted:

"TORPEDOES!"

It had been too late. The bitch had fired before dying. And then massive explosions! We had her! We'd destroyed the bloody Silent. But there was no time for cheers. Our bow was facing the *Herret*.

"COLLISION, SIR!!" That was Valero.

"CORRECT COURSE, MR.VALERO! PORT!!" That was Doorbos.

"What headings, Mr.Steld?!" I called. "The torpedoes! What headings!?"

"It's the *Zelden,* sir! Heading for the *Zelden!*"

There wasn't a doubt in my mind on what to do. The word came out with full confidence.

"Intercept, Mr.Valero."

Valero looked at me, his eyes wide open.

"I'm sorry, sir??"

I faced his stare.

"Intercept those torpedoes, Mr.Valero. Get us side by side with the *Zelden*. Now!"

He did it. And then they were all looking at me. Silent. Incredulous. But they might as well be looking at a rock. Ice cold blood was flowing through my veins. There wasn't an inch of doubt in my mind. The *Zelden* was full of refugees. It was our duty. I could see both torpedoes coming in, now. Closing in. And we were going to make it.

"Gentlemen," I said. "It's been a pleasure serving with you."

And the first one hit us. It hit the bow, just below us, almost immediately destroying the 1st Hull. I had never experienced a force so violent. And then the second one hit us. I don't even know where.

And it all went black.

*I'm coming, Mira. I'm coming… Wait for me.*

\*

HC14 was the first convoy to ever have been subjected to a 'shark attack' – as it became known. From then on, that was the *modus operandi* of the Silent Boats, despite the apparent failure of this first trial. Several of them, sometimes three or four, sometimes more, would converge on a convoy and then would attack with vicious tactics, sometimes days in a row, picking up many merchants and escorts in this manner. For a while, this had a brutal effect and was, in fact, crippling the war effort of Webbur and Torrence. Before the tide turned... We didn't know it at that time, but probes, missiles, and other measures were being developed in Webbur and Torrence in an unprecedented manner, with innovating speed that had not been seen until then and was never seen since. Other detection and communication devices would also play a part. In the end, we mostly beat them with superior technology development capabilities.

The *Loghi* was the first ship in the war to bring down two Silent Boats in one incident. Not many, even at the end of the war, could boast the same. Her tactics when protecting HC14 were studied over and over again, months and years after the convoy reached Webbur – both because of the good decisions and the bad ones. Some of these tactics were employed by others in convoy protection in years to come and may have saved many lives.

I'd like to believe that most of the crew of the frigate understood some of the importance of their performance, what we actually were achieving on that incredible night, even as they plunged into their deaths. But maybe that's just optimism. And maybe I don't even have the right to believe it.

After all, I had just killed them...

# INTERLUDE B – S62

"All right." Said Worf Tinnzer, with his head inside the helmet. "Do we have the targets' ID's confirmed?"

"Yes, *Kapt.* Merchant ship *Solio,* 800k, and merchant ship *Harvy,* 700, are the first."

"Escort?"

"The nearest threat is the *Nyban*, a Corvette. Old class. Not much firepower."

"All right." Worf's helmet showed him the enemy vessels. "Let's not push our luck with the reactor. We get the first two merchants, and we leave."

"Yes, *Kapt.*"

"Time, sir."

"All right. Increase to covert attack speed. Torpedoes?"

"Ready, *Kapt.*"

"63 is engaging, *Kapt.* Position A."

"All right. Rukt, we're deviating. Get us on target."

"Yes, *Kapt.* Sorry, *Kapt.*"

Worf rotated his chair to look at where S63 should be at that point. He had no visual on the other ship, but the friendly ID signal was pulsing a blue dot inside his helmet, so he knew where the other ship was. And also... In a strange move, an enemy ship was getting in an awkward position. It was decreasing speed and falling behind.

'What is that frigate doing?' Thought Worf.

*

Half an hour later, it was all over. Taking his head out of the helmet, Worf was in shock. The mission had been a success. It would be called a success by the brass, he knew it. And S62 had done her duty. It had destroyed three merchant ships. The original first and second targets and a third that had the bad luck of crossing the Silent's crosshairs at the last minute. The Silent had fired a total of six torpedoes, all successful hits.

Those were the good news. The bad news was that S62 was the only survivor attacker on that day. Worf couldn't believe it, but a single frigate had been able to disintegrate two Silent before sacrificing herself to save a merchant ship. It had been an incredible feat. But more than that, what Worf witnessed firsthand was a set of intelligent tactics that would be a danger to Silent Boats all-round. Either that frigate's captain was a genius or, if those had been standard tactics, the Axxian were in trouble.

The crew of S62 was quiet and in shock as well. They hadn't seen, as he'd seen, the enemy frigate in combat, but they knew S60 and S63 were gone. Yet, before Worf could come out of his stupor and say something, the intercom rang, and he picked it up.

"What?"

"It's Karolu, *Kapt.* Permission to shut down the reactor. We're pretty close to danger levels."

"Do it."

He put the comms back in the hanger, looked around and jumped to his feet.

"We need a rendezvous, Urster. Set it up. The reactor won't last. I'll be in my cabin."

"Yes, *Ver-Kaptin.*"

# INTERLUDE C - DEAD

"Stop. Stop." He said softly. "What are you doing?"

I flinched and looked at him. I had sweat dripping from my nose, and my breath was somewhat irregular. I tried to understand what he was telling me. I knew by his soft tone he wasn't happy. He waited for my reply. I stuttered.

"I... I was... Jump, twist, grab the head, throw."

He waved his head.

"It's not what you were doing but how you were doing it. Attitude. Your response must be instinctive, precise, determined. If you hesitate, you're dead. You can't be waiting for me, you have to be open and focused, or the circumstances will overwhelm you. We've been here before. Don't relax."

"But, father... We're just training..."

"Exactly. This is training, not a game. So get serious. Do it right."

"But if I do that, if I'm not careful..."

He waved his head again.

"Stop. Shut up. Shut up." He said, softly. "Just do it."

So I did. I got serious. He attacked me like a bull, or

rather like a stone thrown by a strong arm, directly at my forehead: cold, emotionless, brutal, fast, unstoppable. And I deviated. I was quick. And I jumped, and twisted, and grabbed his head, and threw him to the ground. And I was perfect. Perfect. Victorious. I smiled from ear to ear. I got up, smiling. Happy. But I had been too perfect. And he didn't get up. His body was there, motionless, on the floor. Cold. I lost my smile in half a second.

That's how you lose someone. In half a second.

# EPISODE 4 - RECOVERY

I was awake. I realized it slowly, as if reality was frozen and was unfreezing as I woke up. Slowly, I understood why I was awakening, like that, in the middle of the night. She was there. She was caressing me. Between my legs. And then she cupped my balls. She held them in her hand, for a moment. That left me no doubt I was awake.

The hospital ward was never in the dark. There was always enough light. I looked at her. Brunette, deep blue eyes, nurse uniform, naughty smile, naughty breasts. What was she doing? She started stroking me, and I was erect. Quickly. I inhaled suddenly, inevitably. I was aware others might be awake, just beyond the thin screens she'd closed around my bed. Were they able to feel my breathing? Did she do it to them as well? I looked again. She was looking at me now. With that dirty little smile. And she was pumping. And pumping. Oh, God…

"Don't worry" she whispered, after a while. "I'll clean it up."

She cleaned it up. I didn't say a word. I didn't know what to say. And then she winked at me and left.

What had just happened? I had no idea. Still, she came

back the next Thursday night. And the one after that. Soon, all I had were Thursdays. All I hanged on to was Thursdays.

*

Before the bed, I had been in the 0-gravity ward for several weeks. I had burns in most of my body. My right side, from the neck down, had been burned severely. I had cracked several ribs and many other bones. I had dislocated both shoulders. My face had been pierced by shrapnel on the left side, and I had broken my jaw and lost several teeth. I had a nasty scar on that left side, from my ear to my chin. I had another one on the top of my forehead, from a nasty cut.

I had surgery. They had to reconstruct 40% of my stomach, 50% of my liver and 70% of my right kidney. My right lung had collapsed, but they had been able to get it up and running again.

When I say I had surgery, I don't mean how they do it now. No. Back in those days they actually cut you open. They'd pick up small sharp blades and cut you open, keep you open with a special kind of clamps and put their hands inside you, and metal and plastic things inside you. Of course you're unconscious the whole time, still, it's pretty barbaric by today's standards. But that's how they did it. And they did good work also. Every single damaged internal organ was back to 100% by the time they were done. Those Navy doctors were very good. It was incredible I survived, but it was a real miracle I was able to recover as much as I did.

At least... my body.

*

For weeks I had cried out loud and shouted in the night because of nightmares. I was even violent, a couple of times. I lost the ability to speak. At first, they thought it had been the burns, but soon found out there wasn't really anything wrong physically. I just wasn't talking to anyone. Then they started sedating me and apathy sank in. I would stare at the ceiling all day. I had to be fed through a tube before I started accepting some liquids and soups.

Then one day, Ploom, my old buddy from the *Magnar,* came to see me. He was taken aback when he first saw me. I still had bandages all over my face and head – not to mention most of my body. But he talked and talked, even if I wasn't responding. He said he had spoken to my mother and that she was worried but happy I was alive. It had been a miracle. He said they didn't let her come see me at the Nytar moon, where the military hospital was.

He also spoke of the *Magnar* and all that was going on with my former comrades. Simmas had left, retiring from the Navy because of a medical problem and Orrey had become captain. Usually, he would have been captain of a smaller ship first, but Admiral Hedde had asked for him to stay at the helm of the flagship. That figures. Orrey was good.

Then Ploom started talking about the war. It wasn't going so great. Axx was piling victory after victory all over the inner solar system, and the Silent Boats were still creating havoc inside the Dark Sea and beyond.

And then I spoke. I looked at him and spoke my first words in months:

"Do… Do you know about the *Harvy?*"

"What? The *Harvy?*"

His eyes shined bright, surprised I was speaking.

"My merchant ship. My… The *Harvy.*" I repeated. "Were… were there survivors?"

"I don't know, my friend. I don't know. She was in your convoy? HC14? The merchants weren't too badly hurt. Thanks to you, it seems. I can find out, if you want."

A figment of hope ran through my mind. But I had seen

her explode. There was no hope. I knew that. There was no hope.

"Please. And the *Loghi?*"

"Your ship? The frigate? Well… Almost 90% casualties, I hear. Many wounded but many more dead. You were very lucky. I don't think anyone else in that bridge survived. It was the head of the convoy himself, the destroyer in charge, which came back for you. That captain saved your life."

Yes. Saltz. But it didn't matter. My ship, my first command, was gone. My crew was gone. 90% casualties. And my merchant cow, my baby, the *Harvy,* was gone. And Mirany was gone. Nothing mattered anymore. I wished I had been killed.

But I couldn't tell Ploom that. No. He wouldn't understand.

\*

One day, a high ranking officer came by, with a couple of other people. I didn't respond to anything he said. I'm not sure I even heard him. But he awarded me three medals. The Navy Star of Honor, for my bravery in battle, the Medal of Blood, for my injuries, and the President's Unit of Truth Medal, which was awarded to the whole crew of the *Loghi* – posthumously, for the most part - for having saved others.

For a second, I looked at the officer with surprise, disgust and finally contempt. But after that, I just ignored him, and he left the boxes and the citations on the small table beside my bed. I mean: I had disregarded my orders, I had left my post, I had plunged to death hundreds or thousands of people, and they gave me medals? What were they thinking?

Why couldn't they simply let me die?

\*

At first, I resisted doing physical therapy. But then I found out the punishment made me feel better. The pain was cleansing. So I would push myself much further than they would ask me. Between pain and guilt, pain was better. Between pain and sorrow, pain was better. So I was always asking for more. Always asking the nurses to send me to the gym or the pool. And it hurt. It hurt a lot. Good. Give me more.

\*

There was this nurse called Kary Erbay. Just showed up one day, the fucker. Light brown hair, brown eyes, hard face, cold as fuck. He was a real bastard with me, and every time I did physiotherapy with him, I went further and faster than with any of the others. He was relentless. He almost didn't speak; he just pushed me hard and let me push myself wherever I wanted. I always came back to my bed hurting badly all over.

By this time, most of the bandages had come off, and my scars were showing on my face and body. Red and ugly. And my physical strength was increasing systematically. Still, I was pretty shaken up inside, and still didn't mutter much more than two or three words to anyone.

Erbay started getting the habit of sitting next to my bed when he was on a break. He would do those number puzzles that came in magazines. He would sit by me doing those puzzles and once in a while showing them to me and asking:

"What do you think? A 2 or a 5?"

"Two." I'd say. And he'd check I was right and say:

"Right."

But I had the feeling he wasn't really interested in me. Nor in his puzzles. He never looked at me, not into my eyes. Just analyzed the injuries once in a while. Most of the time he seemed to be observing things around him. People coming and going. He would be with me about an hour a day, and then maybe Estie, my Thursday-night brunette would pass, and he would look at her, quietly, over the magazine, and then stand up and follow her off the room. Or some other nurse would come, and he would observe her going from patient to patient. His behavior was strange, and I started to observe him as well.

He was thirtyish, slim, strong and athletic and his eyes made me feel he had seen combat some time. Also, his walk, straight with his feet slightly pointing to the sides, made me believe he definitely had martial arts training. He was a black belt of something, no doubt. Most people would miss that about him, but I had trained eyes myself, of course. I fantasized he'd been Special Forces, or a Marine Shock Trooper – one of those special units, anyway. What the hell was he doing here? As a nurse?

At one time, Erbay took me to physical therapy. He put me on the walking treadmill, which I still had trouble using. I was walking almost as fast as I could when he said.

"Give me a minute." And he left.

I continued doing my exercise. 5 minutes, 10 minutes. I was getting tired, but there was no sign of Erbay. I was alone in the gym.

"Hey, Erbay!" I called. Nothing.

At 15 minutes I was getting really tired, limping and barely able to walk. I tried to stop the damn machine, but I did just the opposite: it started moving quicker. I tripped and was sent backward violently, bumping my head, with my back flat on the floor. I looked at the ceiling and mentally checked all my body. I wasn't sure it was all intact: I hurt all over, and it was quite possible I had broken some bones. Finally, I tried to get up, but I couldn´t. I crawled to a chair, and that's when Erbay got back and helped me get on my wheel chair.

"WHERE THE FUCK WERE YOU?"

He didn't smile, he didn't look at me, he didn't raise his voice. He seemed perfectly at ease. I had to repeat myself.

"Are you listening, motherfucker? Where the fuck were you?"

"Drinking a beer."

He was pushing my wheel chair by now, and I almost turned and jumped at his neck.

"Drinking a fucking beer!? What are you, a moron!? I could have broken something!!"

"Did you?"

"Fuck you!"

"What do you want me to do? Cry?"

"FUCK YOU!"

We were going through the corridors, by now, and everyone was seeing me losing it while Erbay just kept cool. I wanted to jump from the wheel chair and hit him, but I swear he wouldn't let me. He was just able to steer the chair in such a way I couldn't jump without hurting myself.

"You're a fucking son of a bitch, you know that?"

"Well, yeah." He answered. "But my mother loved me, and that's what counts."

I didn't know what to say after that, so I shut up until we got to my bed. He tried to help me lay down, but I pushed him back.

"Fuck you!"

Finally, I pulled the sheets over my legs, and he folded the wheel chair. He looked me in the eyes and said:

"Why don't you take it easy, from now on?"

"Fuck you."

But as he walked away I was left with that thought in my mind. I thought about it all day and all night. When I woke up the next morning, I had seen his point. I was being silly. I was trying to convince myself and others that I wouldn't care if I got hurt, but that was obviously false. "Fuck him, he took away my punishment," I thought. But even that was idiotic. It seemed there was a limit to the punishment I was ready for. And that was that.

The realization created a void in me. Suddenly, I didn't really know what I wanted, what to strive for. But I started taking it easy, and my physiotherapy sessions got shorter and smoother. Even with Erbay. Soon, I was walking with a cane.

*

One morning, Erbay came by with the wheel chair.

"Come." He said.

"Where?"

"We're going for a walk."

"Don't feel like it."

He pulled the sheets from me before I could grab them.

"Don't care."

He started pulling me to the chair, but I resisted. He was strong, so I pushed my fingers into a special point in his arm, as my father had taught me. He didn't even flinch. It seems I still didn't have all my strength back...

"Not in the mood, Byl." He warned me. I gave up and slid onto the chair.

"Where the fuck are we going?"

He pushed me through the ward.

"Been in the garden?"

"No."

"You'll like it."

"What do I care about a fucking garden?"

"What do I care if you care?"

"Fuck you."

And that was that. We shut up, and he pushed me to the garden.

The garden was a beautiful place, to be honest. The Nytar moon does not have an atmosphere, so everything is indoors. The garden is a big transparent dome that enables us not only to rest within a luxuriant green garden with all kinds of plants but also look into Space and even, like at that very time, see the beauty of Webbur expanding in the sky. I was breathless.

This was the first time I came into the garden, but I would come here many times before I left the hospital. Little by little, I came back to my routine of meditating while looking into space. And I have to say that happened because Erbay brought me there on that day.

The garden was not the last of my surprises, that day, though.

Erbay was pushing me around the compacted dirt paths between the green bushes, and I could hear water running in a fountain. I was baffled, and we didn't speak. Then he made a turn. There was a nice little spot ahead, green grass, a table, peace. Next to the table was an old man in another wheel chair. He had a curved thin but large body, white hair, a stern face, bushy eyebrows, hospital robe and half of a big cigar between his fingers. He pushed the smoke into the high. Erbay took me to the table, beside the old man, he locked in the chair and left. I closed my eyes and breathed deeply, for a moment. That son of a bitch of a nurse was turning me around – fuck him. I had to accept I was enjoying the garden. I even enjoyed the sweet scent of the cigar.

Then the old man, still not looking at me, asked:

"You're Byl Iddo?"

I looked at him. He was Navy, of course. And the cigar told me he was high rank: smoking was strictly forbidden on the hospital grounds.

"Yes, sir."

His deep gray eyes finally plunged into mine.

"I'm Vincenz Cavo."

*

133

Admiral Vincenz Cavo was a legend. He had commanded the three major fleets of Webbur at one time or another and even led the 2nd Fleet to victory in the Pirate Wars. Books had been written about him. Ham Banks, the big movie star, had played him in the award winning motion picture. Still, it took me a few seconds to recognize him from the photographs. He was thinner and more fatigued than seemed possible. His eyes were still sharp and powerful, and the mark of a great man was still visible in his posture and stature. But now he was an old man. Tired and retired.

"I'm honored, sir. I served with your daughter."

"I know, boy. I recommended you."

I remembered. I remembered Mira telling me. I remembered everything about Mira.

"She was the best Captain I ever had."

"What do you mean by 'had'?"

I swallowed hard. That was Vincenz Cavo: a sharp-as-a-razor mind always eager to cut you down. He kept his eyes on the distant stars.

"Well... I mean she was my best Captain ever."

"Were you going to make an honest woman out of her?"

I almost jumped in my chair.

"That's none of your busin..."

I stopped speaking. That was what Mirany would have answered. Stick it to her dad. But I felt something different. I felt the need to share. Share the pain, share the loss. And I was actually facing the only person I could do that with. So I said, with all honesty:

"Yes, sir. I probably was."

He sighed.

"You're a Navy officer. You should have known better."

I looked down at the grass.

"Yes, sir, I should. But she was special."

We didn't say a thing for a few minutes. We just listened to the water fountain playing in the garden, and the distant humming of the air conditioner and the generators.

"The *Harvy*, sir," I said. "Were there any survivors?"

"You were there, I wasn't. You tell me."

I recalled those excruciating moments.

"I saw it explode on the screen. But then I... Then *I exploded.*"

He expelled more smoke into the air.

"She's dead, Byl. Don't hold on to it. There were no survivors."

By 'it' he meant 'hope.' And I felt it escaping, leaving me hollow. The Admiral rested his tired arms on the chair's, his cigar almost finished at the end of his fingers. His head sunk a little inside his shoulders, his eyes searching vaguely the black horizon. He sighed again.

"A reporter once asked me to explain my years, to compare my years: war on one side and my life in peace, with my family, on the other."

The Admiral looked at his hands, as if he held an invisible globe in each.

"Prick. There is no difference. There was no peace, no war, no family. They were all the same thing. I loved the Navy, I was dedicated to it, obsessed by it, fascinated by it. Peace? War? Family? These were circumstances that happened, eventualities that punctuated my long sick love affair with the Navy."

I looked at him. There was a strange energy coming from his voice. Deep. Strong.

"I lost friends." He continued. "Comrades. Closer to me than brothers. I lost them out there, in the Dark Sea. No glory. None. Glory is for others, for the naïve, the ignorant, the politicians, the poets. No glory. Just that shit we know is up there. That void. That sickening void. You know what I mean, don't you, Lieutenant?"

"Yes, sir. I do."

"It's stupid to say that it was a surprise to lose my daughter. I knew she was out there. I knew what it meant. I knew what she was getting into. But still, it was a surprise. The consequences were a surprise. What I felt... What I lost..."

My heart was pumping inside my chest. His pain was so real... So real... As real as mine. As real as something that was creeping up inside me. A black tide rising from the depths.

And then the Admiral said:

"But I still love the Navy, heavens help me."

And my voice came out, saying:

"Me too..."

I closed my eyes and lowered my head. And I heard him again, after puffing the cigar:

"Just two sick, sad fuckers, aren't we, Mr.Iddo?"

"Yes, sir."

And I cried. Tears came flowing. I tried to sob silently, not to moan, not to sniff. I did my best. But I cried. For several minutes that was all that happened. I had my eyes closed, and my hands on my face and my mind sinking in a black tide, trying desperately to swim.

I cried. There. Beside him. And then I stopped. My hands fell into my lap. And for a few minutes, we were there, just listening to the water, the AC, the generators. Just breathing,and remembering. I closed my eyes again, feeling my face wet and cold.

I finally heard a 'blip' from an intercom. The one he had on the lapel of his robe. And when I opened my eyes, Erbay was approaching. He unlocked the Admiral's chair and turned it to take him away. Cavo threw the cigar into the bushes with a push from a finger and looked at me.

"See you tomorrow, lieutenant."

"Yes, sir," I replied. "Certainly, sir."

*

The next day, Erbay came and took me to the garden again. To the table on the grass, where Cavo was expecting me.

"Thanks, Kary." He said to Erbay, as the nurse walked away. I noticed then there was a special relationship between them. Not really sure what kind.

"Sleep well?" Asked the Admiral.

"Yes, sir. Thank you." I had. Actually, I hadn't slept as well as that night for weeks. Since I had been sedated.

"Good. You need your rest."

He picked up a cigar from his pajama's pocket and lit it. I looked at him.

"Why are you here, sir?"

He smiled.

"Liver. Will die eventually. God knows when. But until then I have to get regular treatments. A week or so every few months."

"I'm sorry."

"Bah… Something will get you sooner or later. So it's the liver. Could be worst."

"Like what?"

He raised his eyebrows.

"I don't know. Fuck… The head, I guess."

I looked at the grass.

"How did you know Mirany and I were involved?"

He expelled smoke.

"Are you serious? Do you think I wouldn't keep an eye out for my little girl?"

"We were discrete."

He giggled.

"Like elephants. But don't worry about it. The Navy doesn't know. She doesn't know what she doesn't want to know."

I looked up. The Brury moon was rising on the other side of Webbur, its pearly white color striking against the black scenery.

"That lady is a beauty." He said, looking at it as well. I sighed and nodded.

"They gave me medals," I said.

"Take them." He answered.

"You don't understand. What happened is… I disobeyed orders. People died because of me. A frigate was 'sunk.' Thousands of people."

"Bullshit." He paused. He took the smoke in and out. "Want to know what happened that day? Two convoys were hit. Two convoys hit on the same day by several Silent Boats at the same time. They call it 'shark attacks.' It's their new M.O. So, two convoys, one of them lost 18 ships, the other lost 5. Guess which one was yours."

My mouth was wide open from the surprise.

"18?"

"The average is 16.5 ships lost per convoy since it began. It's a mess. No convoy suffered a 'shark attack' and lost less than 10 ships. Except HC14. If you ask me, you deserve those medals. So put your mind at ease, boy, and forget about it. They look good on the uniform anyhow."

I looked down.

"Captain Saltz, sir?"

"What?"

"I expect they must have talked to Captain Saltz, the convoy's C.O., over this, sir. He wouldn't have been too happy that I…"

"Oh, shut up, lieutenant!" He was losing his patience. "Saltz is a bit rigid and slow to react, but he is sound. Who do you think suggested you for the medals in the first place?"

"He…?"

"Just forget about it. Swallow the medals and leave it be. Is that so hard?"

"No, sir."

"There, then. For fuck's sake…"

And we were a few more minutes in silence. Looking at the stars. Side by side.

"The war, sir?" I eventually asked.

"What about it?"

"How's it going?"

"Not that great. The fortress moons of Torrance have been able to hold and keep Axx's forces away, but they still are surviving thanks to our provisions, as long as they last. The 1st *Vüurkorps* has been sent to occupy Haitzia. Along with 18 million *Stürm* soldiers. Ambitious bastards, aren't they?"

Hatzia is the big planet on the other side of the sun. Its position and orbit is completely symmetrical to Webbur's, so the planet is never seen directly from our position. It is also rich in cereals and minerals, but it has a colder core, so about 30% of its surface is permanently frozen. It boasts numerous and tough even if unsophisticated military forces that are fanatics in their continuous attack tactics. But I wouldn't envy their task. The 1st Fleet of Axx, the 1st *Vüurkorps*, was a solid unit and the *Stürm* troopers were some of the hardest and better-trained land and sea fighters in the system. And if Axx got hold of Haitzia, it would have an important source of supplies that would be very important to fight the rest of the war. Still, the fact that Axx was confident enough to attack Haitzia was scary on its own. After all, it was a distant planet, separated from Axx by the Eeron and the Mirox asteroid belts and the Dark Sea; invading it wasn't a small feat.

"Torrance's main fleet has been dispatched to intercept it, so it will be a hell of a battle." The Admiral spat off a piece of leave the cigar had left on his tongue.

Torrance's Great Royal Fleet had once been the mightiest fleet in the known Universe. She had become a lot smaller since then, and most of her ships were much older than they should be. Still, it was a very important asset, and the Battle of Haitzia would be one of the most critical of the war.

"A hell of a battle…" I mumbled.

"But that's not the damn battle that worries me, lieutenant. Not at all. Believe me, that's not the battle that's going to decide the fate of this war."

"What then, sir?"

He sniffed and moved his tongue around his teeth.

"The Dark Sea Battle. That's the one. That's the direst of them all. It scares the hell out of me."

I looked directly at him. He wasn't joking. He continued.

"If our convoys don't hold, Torrance is done. They have at the most 3 to 4 months of provisions on their own. So convoys must continue. Still, at the rate we're losing ships, we have an ability of perhaps 6 more months of maintained supply. And with the winter here, the route to Torrance is now lasting around 10 weeks so the convoys will be longer in the danger zone for the next few months. Our best hope is for the 2nd Fleet to get into the Dark Sea and fight off the Silent Boats. The Fleet has been reinforced, and the SB's have no chance against her now, I believe."

"So, why doesn't she? Why isn't the 2nd Fleet entering the Dark Sea for the hunt?"

He expelled a cloud of smoke.

"Because that's the trap. That's what the *Addmiralis* is expecting we do. The 2nd *Vüurkorps* has been upgraded with serious fire power and is waiting for the 2nd Fleet there, on the edge of the Dark Sea. Two new 1st-tier warships, the *Assauer* and the *Serdal Kuo*, have joined the enemy fleet, and they are a whole lot of trouble. And even if we are able to defeat them all, which I believe we are, a wounded 2nd Fleet would be easy prey for the *Styllemarinne*. The Silent's *shark attacks* are very deadly to wounded ships, even for big beasts like ours, as you might imagine. Especially if the *Vüurkorps* is able to damage many or most of our destroyers and frigates. No. The 2nd Fleet needs to wait."

"But wait for what, sir?"

He looked at me. His gaze reminded me of some kind of predator.

"For an edge, lieutenant. For an edge."

"An edge, sir?"

"Yes. We need to find an edge against the Silent. Against the sharks. Then, the 2nd Fleet can go into the Dark Sea."

I didn't know which kind of edge he thought we could get against the Silent. Still, there was something else that was intriguing me even more.

"How do you know all this, sir? I thought you were retired."

He smiled.

"No one can be retired in a war like this. No. They still have some use for me."

"But much of what you're telling me is surely classified, sir. How is it you are telling it to me?"

He smiled some more and pressed the button on his intercom.

"Because you'll need to know, lieutenant. Because you'll need to know."

What the hell was he talking about? At that moment, Erbay came out of the bushes to pick up the Admiral. The old man winked at me as he was being pushed away.

"Let's speak some more in a few days, shall we, lieutenant?"

"Yes, sir."

And the son of a bitch left me there completely baffled.

\*

At this time, I was surprised that they hadn't discharged me already. All the health indicators were coming up to normal, and I could almost walk without a cane, just limping a little bit. When I asked, they told me to wait a few more days. Until eventually I wrote a letter. But never got an answer.

It wasn't as if I had somewhere to go. I would go home, I'd expect, my mother's home, but after that, who knew? Still, I was sick and tired of the hospital (no pun intended). I needed to get out of there, and I needed to get out of there soon.

\*

For the past few weeks, Nurse Eiste had been missing our implicit Thursday-night standing date. I didn't know why it stopped. But as I also didn't know why it had begun, that wasn't a big surprise. I expected she had found some other lucky idiot to have fun with.

That night, however, I was awoken by a familiar touch. I felt her hand crawling underneath the sheets. Caressing my leg. I looked at her. She smiled. Her naughty blue eyes finding mine in the duskish light. I felt her fingers on my testicles and jumped inside, becoming rigid. I wanted to say something, to welcome her back, but we'd never spoken in these encounters, and it felt strange and bothersome to say something. I lifted my hand and rested it on her round buttock, and that was the best I could do to acknowledge her.

I felt her moving, down there, and started to breathe deeper and faster. But I don't know why this time I wasn't up to a cold mechanical encounter. I raised my hand up to her waist and pulled her to me. She resisted at first, but then she raised herself and was looking right into my eyes, her breasts sitting on my chest, her mouth close to mine. She had beautiful eyes. Eyes get me every time. Her hand was still moving down there, but I stopped her and pulled her further. She didn't want to kiss me, I don't know why, but finally, she did. We kissed. Gently. I smoothly sucked her upper lip, then the bottom one. Then we separated. She was still resisting.

I felt something strange, then. My hand was on her waist, her right hand was now supporting her on the bed, but I felt the left arm moving, doing something. She looked into my eyes and noticed I noticed it, so she kissed me hard and passionate. I kissed her back, but now my attention was focused on the movement of her arm. She was doing something. She was distracting me while her left hand was doing something below my bed, underneath my mattress. What was she doing?

We kissed for a few minutes, and finally, she smiled awkwardly, kissed me again with a bit of tongue, then backed away and left.

I stayed awake for a while, looking at the dark ceiling. In part, I was satisfied and even a bit elated. The making out had been more satisfying than a hand job would have been. On the other hand, I was sure it had been awkward. All of it. It had been very awkward. Even more than usual. What was she doing with me? What was she doing in my bed? What was she doing *underneath* my bed? And did I care?

Finally, I made a decision, turned around in the bed and searched with my hand beneath it. It took me a while, but finally, I found it. It was a small compartment in the metal, in the structure of the bed. It had a tiny sliding door, and there was something in there. I took it out. In the dark, I could barely perceive it, but it was a black piece, some kind of chip, some kind of memory chip. That was strange. That was very strange. I thought about it for a long time, but in the end, I put it in my pajama's pocket and went to sleep. Whatever this was, it was way over my head.

*

Friday morning, Erbay took me to the Admiral once

again. I asked the old man:

"Do you know Nurse Eiste?"

He nodded.

"Your Thursday-night hand job?"

Son of a bitch! How the hell did he know that?! I braced myself and kept quiet, not to give him the satisfaction. Son of a bitch! But I did have something he didn't know about. I was sure. I took out the memory chip and showed it to him.

"Yes, my Thursday-night booty call," I said. "Turns out she was hiding this little thing in my bed."

He raised his eyebrow. I *had* surprised him.

"You should put it back." He said.

"Know what it is?"

He looked straight at me, which meant it was serious.

"Nurse Eiste's real name is Nina Zauer, she's an enemy spy. That little thing you have there, is a chip containing a top-secret level 1 Navy code. She's hiding it until she is able to get it out across the Dark Sea."

What the hell!? My mouth opened wide and I was speechless. Who the hell was this old man!? How did he...? An enemy spy? A top-secret code? What was this? This was dangerous. I looked around, making sure no one was listening.

"What the hell, sir!"

He smiled.

"Don't worry. We're secure here. Erbay is making sure of that."

I looked at him.

"Who are you?"

He laughed.

"I'm still a Navy Admiral, lieutenant. But they've put me in charge of a special unit no one really talks about."

"A special unit?"

"Navy Intelligence. We call ourselves The Farmers."

"You mean... I..." I didn't know what to say. I

looked at the black chip in my hand. "You want me to put this back?"

He put a cigar in his mouth.

"Don't worry, lieutenant. It's not a real code. It's a fake one. And it would be very interesting to see how Nurse Eiste intends to take it to the enemy."

I looked at the chip, and then back at him.

"So… You're here because… Your liver…"

"No. I'm really sick. I didn't have to come all the way here for my treatment, of course, but my sickness is real."

"Why *The Farmers?* Because you seed things and see them play out?"

He laughed again.

"No, nothing so fancy. They've set up our HQ in a farm somewhere in Ollory, that's all. We've been The Farmers ever since."

"Is Erbay one of yours?"

He nodded.

"One of the best. He's in charge of the whole operation, really. I'm just here to oversee and, well… to meet you, in truth."

I thought for a bit, then I raised the chip in my hand.

"So I put it back?"

He nodded again.

"I'd appreciate it. Discreetly, if you don't mind. And fast."

"Very well." I got it back to my pocket. "You're putting a lot of trust in me, telling me all this."

He smiled.

"I've been studying you for a long time."

Oh… Now I understood what he was doing.

"So you're recruiting me? Is that it?"

He took his cigar to his mouth, smiling widely and reminding me of Mira.

"Pretty much, yes."

I thought about it for a bit. He just smoked the cigar

and waited, the old fox.

"I don't think I'm secret agent material," I said.

"You are, but that's beside the point: I don't need you as an agent."

I raised my eyebrows.

"You don't?"

He clicked the button on his intercom.

"Let's do the following, shall we, Byl? You go put that chip back, and we'll talk again after that, what do you say?"

Erbay showed up. The Admiral was going to leave me hanging, as usual.

"Off you go." I joked. "Work the land, milk the cows, harvest the crop…"

Erbay raised an eyebrow, uncomfortable with my impertinence, but the Admiral laughed.

"Sunrise to sunset, boy! Sunrise to sunset!"

*

I went back to my bed. I didn't immediately return the chip to its hiding place because it was the middle of the day and there were many people around, wide awake and active. I had to wait for a moment when nobody would notice my action, of course.

But I didn't have the chance.

Yohan was a nurse I didn't know very well. He was detached to a different ward, and he seldom came by. Which was why I was surprised when he showed up with a wheel chair.

"Byllard Iddo, right?"

"Yes. Lieutenant." I didn't know him well enough to let him ignore my rank.

"Right. Come." He unfolded the chair.

He was a big guy. Dark hair, dark eyes, dark face. He was fit. Navy fit. And very physical.

"Where are we going?" I asked, as he pushed me

through the corridors.

Silence. He didn't say a word. I started to feel alarmed, somehow. Where the hell were we going? Finally, he turned the chair into an empty corridor and then into a mid-sized almost empty storage room. He stopped in the middle and waited. I was ready to get up, but he calmly but firmly put a hand on my shoulder. I didn't have to wait long, anyway. After a few seconds here came Nina Zauer a.k.a. Nurse Eiste. Now I really wanted to get up, and now I really knew it wouldn't be that easy. I looked at Eiste. She did look good in that nurse's uniform, heavens help me. She had lipstick on. I'm serious. Red lipstick, the slut.

She showed me the little device. It was a Star-Thrower. A small two-barrel pistol that shoots two heavy star shaped slow moving round bullets. The beastly thing wasn't able to hit an elephant further than 15 to 20 palms away, but it could devastate what it hit.

"Know what it is?" Eiste asked.

I nodded.

"Know what it can do to you?"

I nodded again.

"Your insides get torn apart." She explained anyway. "Not a pretty thing."

I waited. She smiled coldly.

"Know that tiny black thing I hid in your bed?" She asked.

"Tiny black thing?" I said with fake naïveté.

"You took it, and I need it back."

I thought for a bit, trying to figure out how to play this. But I finally took the chip from my pocket and gave it to her. She inspected it.

"What is it, anyway?" I asked.

She just nodded at Yohan with intent and then left without even looking at me. Yohan started pushing me again, in the opposite direction.

"Don't even try to get up." He said, with a grave voice.

147

"Or I'll kill you right here."

I believed him, so I stayed still, looking for an opening. Before it came, we went through a door saying 'Crematorium,' and I got cold sweat all over.

The room was mostly dark. There were about six stretchers with dead bodies on them, covered in white sheets, just there waiting for something, and a large oven with huge yellow flames illuminating the place.

"What are we doing here, Yohan?"

Yohan didn't answer. He guided me to the center of the room and locked wheels. And then everything happened in a flash.

I tried to get up, but he grabbed my shoulder. I put my knee down, slipping off the chair, rotated over the knee, grabbed his arm and pushed his elbow towards his ear as I got up, unbalancing him against a stretcher. He was surprised by my skill, but quickly recovered and threw me a potent hook with his right fist. But I was expecting it since my unbalancing act left him with only one direction to strike, so I ducked clean. Exactly as I wanted! As I ducked, I closed my left hand in a praying-mantis fist and fired it into his liver. My body wasn't really in the proper position to be accurate, but I knew my craft, and I compensated in a split second. A strike to the liver is something brutal. Yohan didn't even shout. His knees shook. His face was a mask of pain. I knew he wouldn't be thinking right at that point. He wouldn't even be seeing right. And before he could recover, my right hand's palm crashed violently against his nose. He stumbled back and fell on his knee. He was near unconsciousness already. I jumped forward. He tried to catch my arm, but I slapped his hand away. I grabbed the hair on the top of his head firmly and pulled it back, while I pushed his chin with the other hand, he was unbalanced again, and I rotated my hips pushing the head and pulling the chin, and when I freed him, he was sent flying a dozen palms away. He crashed into the open oven door, and his head exploded into a pool of blood. Just like that, he was dead. And worst of all, his hair caught fire. It was so gruesome and stupid that I immediately pulled a sheet from one of the dead bodies and attacked the flames like a madman until they were out. And fuck, fuck, fuck! It was over...

I sat on the ground next to the body. I closed my eyes and took deep breaths for a moment. I calmed myself down. When I opened my eyes, I looked around. The whole place was a mess. What should I do with the body? I had to make Yohan disappear. I knew that. It was important that Eiste didn't know that he was dead and I was alive until she left. I knew that. But I wasn't sure of what to do. I could burn the body, clean the place with the sheet, burn the sheet. But what if I did something wrong? What if I left clues all over the place? They'd charge me with murder, wouldn't they? The best thing was to get help. The best thing was to get Erbay. He would know what to do.

I dragged Yohan's body and hid it behind a metallic counter. I put the sheet over the body to hide it a little more. Just enough so it wasn't noticed right away by somebody who'd come by or something. I didn't touch the blood. I just thought I would create a bigger mess if I tried to clean it up.

I walked out of the Crematorium trying to figure out how to find Erbay. I could try and ask somebody to call him. But that might alert Eiste or somebody else if they happened to hear it. And who could I trust? I decided instead to wander through the corridors until I find him. With hindsight, that was even dumber. I could have been spotted by a number of enemy agents if they were there. Finally, I passed a room that had an oxygen bottle and a mask. I snatched it, put the mask on, so I would be a little more disguised, and sat down in a corner of one of the main corridors, waiting for Erbay to come by. It took at least half an hour. I spotted him and called him up. He looked at me, and looked at the mask and asked:

"What the hell are you doing?"

"Something happened," I said, mysteriously.

He raised his eyebrow.

"Come. Let's talk over there. And leave the damn bottle, will you?"

He took me to an empty room, and I told him everything.

"Show me." He said.

I took him to the Crematorium and showed him the body. Despite my fears over the last hour, nobody seemed to have found Yohan while I was gone. Everything was exactly in the same place as before.

"What do we do?" I asked.

His face betrayed no emotion.

"You will go back to your bed and lay low. I'll take care of this."

I tried to protest.

"I could help y…"

"I'll get to you when I get to you." He interrupted.

"But I just…"

"Go."

His finger was indicating the exit. His eyes left me with no doubt that I'd better go. And so I went… As simple as that. Like nothing had happened at all. Like I hadn't killed a man or something. Like I hadn't almost been killed myself or something. Just like that. Just back to my bed and look at the ceiling. Fucking spooks.

\*

The next morning, Erbay took me back to the garden.

"Good job." Said the Admiral, playing with his cigar.

We were next to the fountain, and I had my hand in the water, playing.

"Is she gone?"

"Yes."

"Are you following her?"

"We have a tracking device."

"Won't they scan the chip?"

He smiled.

"It's not in the chip. We know what we're doing, lieutenant."

I lowered my eyes.

"Sorry, sir."

He coughed a little.

"What were you thinking of doing after this?"

Here we go...

"Back to my mother's house, I guess. I'm not going back to convoys, that's for sure."

He sniffed.

"Your father died when you were... what? Sixteen?"

I looked up.

"Yes, sir."

"An accident?"

"Yes, sir."

"You killed him in training?"

I stopped. That wasn't a real question; he knew the truth. But it hurt to hear it out loud. It felt like a burning iron coming out of my gut.

"Yes, sir," I whispered.

"You blame yourself?"

I had thought of it for years. Nothing I could have done. I'd done what my father ordered. And I'd done it well. However...

"I don't, and I do, sir." I sighed.

"Your mother blames you?"

He was relentless.

"She doesn't, but she does."

He chewed the cigar.

"Tough spot, aren't you? Guilt is a bitch. So the Navy became your family, did she?"

"I guess so, sir."

"The big dark Space lured you in, did it?"

151

"I suppose so, sir."

"It hurts you, and it squashes you, but you can't leave it, can you?"

My fingers played with the water in the fountain. There are no fountains in Space. There's nothing in Space. It's empty. And that's what gets you; it has space for you.

"Come work for me." He said finally.

"Doing what, sir?"

He blew some smoke into the heights.

"The Silent boats are being able to cover the entire Dark Sea not because they have that kind of functioning range, but because they have ways of re-supplying deep in Space. There is this ship… We call it The Mother. It works as a hub for the sharks: it supplies them and in a way, commands them. It's a fake merchant, well armed and big enough to be nasty. It travels the Dark Sea somewhere near the Pirate Zone. It works with two or three other supply Silent Boats that can make it even more efficient. So what the SB's have is not a functioning range but an operating range enabled by this bitch. If we can find her and kill her, we cut their range in half."

"I see… So…"

"Yes. Your Nurse Eiste will be going to the Pirate Zone, probably land in Fumu itself. But then she will arrange transport to The Mother. That's how valuable she thinks her product is. That's how valuable the enemy thinks her product is. Erbay and his team will follow her all the way. I have procured a ship and a crew to take him there and do the dirty job of destroying that fucking monster, and I would very much like for you to command her."

My heart stopped at that moment. I felt I was trembling all over. My teeth were clenched. It was a mix of fear, excitement, and amazement. If I had been conscious of myself, I would probably have felt an erection downstairs. The Admiral smiled dangerously and continued.

"Priority One of the mission is to destroy The Mother

and as many of her supply-SB's as possible. Priority Two is, if possible, board the bitch, secure an encrypting machine codenamed *Libra*, in which all Silent Boat communication is managed so they can do 'shark attacks,' and leave without the enemy ever knowing we've got it."

My mouth was dry. My hands were sweating. He finished with an almighty sentence:

"Do this, and the 2nd Fleet can go into the Dark Sea and turn this whole fucking war around."

He put the cigar in his mouth and smoked, waiting, while my mind was jumping all over the place like a ping-pong ball. This was big. This was really big.

"That… The mission…" I started to say.

"Yes?"

"It sounds dangerous."

He laughed out loud and chewed the cigar.

"It's borderline suicidal!"

And, as he was laughing that devil's laugh, that power-hungry danger-addict Navy-crazy scary manipulator's laugh, I said:

"I can see why she hated you."

That was stupid! I knew it the moment I said it. That was a stupid, stupid thing to say. I could see his face turning into stone. The pain so obvious in his eyes. So real. What a stupid thing to say!

"I'm sorry, sir… What I meant was…"

I had to say something. Something honest. Something sincere. From the heart. I said:

"She loved you as well, sir. Very much. She resented you, yes, but she really loved you."

His eyes were different now. Cold. Distant. He said:

"Well? Are you doing this or not?"

And I knew the answer already:

"Yes, sir. I am."

He pressed the button.

"Good. Erbay will set you up. Be ready for him."

153

Erbay came out of the bushes and unlocked the Admiral's chair.

"I'm sorry, sir," I said.

"It's alright, lieutenant. Don't worry about it."

It wasn't alright, but there was nothing else I could do. I saw them leave and then I got up and returned to bed on my own.

\*

On my night stand, next to the bed, was an unfamiliar envelope somebody had left for me. I opened it. It was my discharge papers. It seems my doctors had deliberated and decided I could leave at my convenience. Yeah, right... Nice timing.

I didn't really know how to get ready for Erbay. I just picked up all my stuff and shoved it into my bag. Finally, I left it under my bed and went to the library. Had just thought of something.

I came back to my bed soon afterward and ended up waiting for Erbay the rest of the day. He showed up when I was dozing off before dinner. He kicked my bed, just strong enough so I'd wake up. And I did. And looked at him.

"Pick you up tomorrow morning. 0700."

"That late, hein?" I joked. 7 a.m. was kind of tardy for the Navy, in fact. I guess I'd sleep late.

"Just be ready."

"Sure."

"Uniform, I mean."

"Okay."

"Not a word to anybody."

"Fine."

"And don't be cocky."

"Fuck you."

I had been ready for the last few weeks, actually. The fucking spook went away, and I closed my eyes again.

\*

0700 hours. We were leaving a bit later than would be natural because the Admiral wanted to say goodbye to me. I'm glad he did.

"I'm sorry for what I said yesterday," I told him.

"Don't worry about it." He smiled. "You're family, and family members say these things to each other once in a while. That's how it works, I guess."

I didn't know if he was being honest or not, but I assumed he was. Anyway, he was trying to be nice. I was moved. I gave him the book.

"Here. Some poetry. This was her favorite author."

He picked it up and looked at it as if it was a strange thing.

"From the library?" He smiled.

"I don't expect they'll go find me out there for the return." I smiled back.

"Don't be so sure…" He joked. "Thank you, Byl." He said. And he meant it. He'd liked the gesture. He looked into my eyes. "You understand your orders will be verbal only? You cannot take into the ship anything that will identify you."

"Yes, sir."

"You will be at Commander Erbay's orders. You're the captain of the ship, but he's the mission's CO and the mission comes first, is that clear?"

"Perfectly, sir."

"Your ship is the *Arrabat*. It's an adapted sloop-of-war." He sat back. "In the old days, when we were still sailing on water, sloops were led by a particular rank. 'Masters and commanders.' Knew that?"

"Not really, sir."

"That's before 'commander' became a rank on its own." He played with the unlit cigar in his hand. "You will be captain of the *Arrabat*, but officially you'll be promoted to commander, is that clear?"

"Yes, sir."

In truth, I hadn't even thought of a promotion. There were no ranking commanders in frigates or lesser ships. Commanders were ranking officers in larger warships.

"You'll receive better pay, pension, and benefits."

"That's good, sir."

"Your mother will get that if you don't return."

"That's good, sir."

He paused and looked at me with concern.

"Be careful out there, commander."

I smiled.

"I will, sir."

"Listen to Erbay. He knows what he's doing. He'll train you on the way. Listen to everything he says."

"I will, sir."

"She's a good ship. Swift and smart. You'll like her. "

"I'm sure I will, sir."

"I picked out your officers myself. And all the men were screened by my people."

"Thank you, sir."

"So you'll probably have a tight ship."

"That'll be great, sir."

"Well…" He raised his frail hand. I got to my feet and shook it, as firmly as I could without harming him. "So long, commander. Off you go."

"Yes, sir."

"Work the land, milk the cows…"

"Harvest the crop." I finished. "Sunrise to sunset, sir. Sunrise to sunset."

We smiled at each other. I saluted. He saluted back. And off I went.

# INTERLUDE D - SURVIVOR

Mirany understood the *Harvy* was in terrible trouble as soon as the second contact was announced. She had never heard of two Silent attacking a convoy at the same time, much less three. Inside a second, she thought of me, out there in the *Loghi*, she thought of her crew, but then she thought of the thousands of refugees holding each other in the bottom of the hulls.

"Torpedo! Going for the *Fott*, Captain!"

The *Fott* was right behind the *Harvy*. Mira looked back and saw the explosion being carried all the way towards them.

"Hold on!"

The ship shook violently. And then came the shrapnel.

"Damages!?"

"Hull 5 is badly hit, Captain!"

"Captain!" Called Zhany. "We don't have comms with hulls 4 and 6!"

And Mira didn't even hesitate.

"Zhany, you have the bridge! You know what to do! Krytia! With me!"

Mira and Krytia went down to the deck and climbed

on a transport kart. In seconds, they were speeding towards the stern.

"I'm leaving you on 4." Said Mirany. "Get the escape pods ready and organized. Children first. Got that?"

"Yes, Captain!"

The kart stopped next to H4's gate, and Krytia stepped out. Mira grabbed her arm.

"Krytia! Thank you."

And that was a goodbye. That was the moment Krytia realized the *Harvy* was not going to survive.

"Thank you, Captain." She replied.

Mira accelerated the kart, and she never saw Krytia again.

\*

Wolton, a short, thin young man, was the captain of Hull 6. He greeted Mira two seconds before the ship shook violently again from more impacts. They both held to the walls.

"Bad, Captain?" He asked, a few seconds later.

"Pretty bad, Captain Wolton." Replied Mira with a soft smile. "We'll be targeted very soon. We need to get the pods ready."

Wolton went pale. And then he nodded. He took Mira across the hull, towards the emergency escape pods, giving orders left and right to any crew member he met on the way.

"Children first." Reminded Mira, as they arrived next to the pod marked 6.3.

"Yes, Captain." Smiled Wolton. "We have it covered."

She looked back and saw a few children coming through one after the other, grabbing the shoulders of the ones in front. Wolton opened the pod door, while crew members guided the refugees inside.

"You have all the pods online?"

Wolton nodded.

"All fifteen."

"How many people?"

"We figure 150."

Mira swallowed hard. 150 people was less than 15% total. Less than 15% of all refugees would survive, let alone the crew of the *Harvy*. She looked at Wolton.

"One adult per pod. We need to do this quic..."

And that's when the first torpedo hit them.

*

Mira woke up with a piercing headache. She had several pairs of eyes looking at her closely. Oh, the headache! There wasn't much light around, but she finally could see the children around her. She was inside an escape pod. She looked back. The door was closed. The pod had been launched!

"Are you okay?"

One, two, three, four children. Between the ages of four or five and ten or eleven. Most of them, crying.

"How many...? I'm fine. How many of you... of us here in the pod?"

"Ten, miss." Replied the oldest girl. "They've put six of us in those drawers over there."

She pointed to the cryo-cribs in the walls. Mira swallowed hard. There was real danger in cryogenics. Especially for children. She tried to get up, slowly. The headache seemed to prey on her, to lean against her, but she resisted. She picked herself up. The little girl, the oldest one, held her arm, helped her up. Mira smiled at her, thanking her. She wanted to give comfort to the crying ones, tell them that everything was alright, but first, she had to see. She had to know. She approached the wide thin watch at the front of the pod. She was going to look out when suddenly she saw a shadow. Something coming from the starboard side, very close, getting between the sunlight and the small escape pod. A ship.

She looked, while her hand immediately picked up the emergency microphone. And then she froze. She looked out, and it was a Silent. An enemy ship. A slender dark figure. Very close, moving slowly, even though slowly, for small ships in Space, was too fast... She looked around very quickly. There wasn't any other vessel around. None she could immediately see. She looked down, pressed the buttons, checked the sensors. Nothing close. She knew she couldn't miss it. She knew she couldn't miss the contact. It was dangerous either way, and she had to make the right choice. She clicked on the mike.

"Emergency, emergency! This is Emergency Escape Pod 6.3 from Webbur merchant ship *Harvy*. Do you hear me?"

Silence. No one responded. Mira could hear the children crying quietly behind her. She looked back. They were all in a corner. The oldest girl was closer to her. Looking up at her. Awaiting instructions.

"What's your name?" Asked Mirany, softly.

"Hedder... But they call me Hedi." Said the little brown-haired girl, no more than twelve years old.

"Hedi... I'm Mira. Could you help me with them?" Mira nodded towards the other children. "We're gonna be okay. Could you help your friends?"

Hedi tried to smile and gave a little nod, before turning around and go comforting the others. Mira turned to the mike once more.

"Emergency, emergency! This is Emergency Escape Pod 6.3 from Webbur merchant *Harvy*. Do you hear me?"

Silence. She sighed and tried once more.

"Emergency, emergency! This is Emergency Escape Pod 6.3 from Webbur merchant *Harvy*. Do you hear me?"

And this time, she felt a click in the mike. A response.

"Who is this?"

An Axxian voice. A straight, cold accent.

"This is Emergency Escape Pod 6.3 from Webbur merchant *Harvy*." She repeated. "Do you hear me? We need assistance."

There was a law of Space. A law of assistance. Every vessel had to help one another. Even in war. Escape pods were helped. Taken in. They would be prisoners, but alive. Survivors. But then the other responded.

"I'm sorry, Emergency Escape Pod 6.3. We cannot help you."

This was what she feared. Silent Boats had limited supplies. And they had missions. They didn't take prisoners. There was the law. But they were outside it. They didn't take any prisoners.

"Please! Can you identify yourself?" Asked Mira, feeling a sliver of desperation. "We have children on board!"

Maybe that would turn them. Maybe that would change their minds. There were children! In the name of all that's sacred! There were children!

But then she heard the words:

"Good luck."

And that was it. The Silent was gone.

*

Mira turned to the children. They packed together against the back wall, looking miserable. Hedi was the oldest. There was also a boy of about 8 or 9, and two others, obviously brother and sister, of about 5 years old. Mira sighed.

"Hi. I'm Mirany. And who are you? I know Hedi. But how about you?"

The children looked at her, frightened. It was Hedi who made the introductions, in a tired tone.

"This is Jona. He's 8. And these are Uny and Goy. They are twins." She turned to the younger ones. "How old are you? Six?"

"Five…" Whispered Uny, the little girl, showing an open hand.

"Nice to meet you." Smiled Mira. "Well, here we are. I'm a Captain. This is our ship. You must be the crew, right?"

The children looked at each other, puzzled. Mira continued.

"Let me see. Hedi will be my X.O., my second in command. You know what that means, Hedi?"

The girl looked confused.

"No, mom."

"It means that if I happen to be asleep, or I'm not around for some reason, you're in charge. Every one okay with that?"

The kids nodded silently. Mira looked around.

"What do you think of our ship?"

Goy said something almost no-one could hear.

"What did you say?" Asked Mira.

The little girl stepped in for her brother beside her.

"He says the ship is a little bit tiny."

Mira smiled.

"Yes, she is. Do you think we can handle her?"

The children nodded affirmatively again.

"How's she called?" Asked Jona.

"The ship?" Replied Mira. "So far, she's called Emergency Escape Pod 6.3. What do you think? Should we give her another name?"

They looked at each other, timid.

"Maybe… Maybe we could call her Janny?" Suggested Uny.

"Janny. Sounds good. Who votes 'yes'?"

Everyone raised their hands.

"Very well." Concluded Mira. "From now on, our ship's name is Janny. Should we get to know her?"

\*

The Escape Pod *Janny* was a small vessel with two different levels. In all the escape pods of the *Harvy* Mira had installed some features that made vessels like these considerably better than average. One of these features was the new, even though expensive, adhesive graviton floors. They gave the crew a sense of weight and attached a person to the floor, even though it made it difficult to move, as if the floor was sticky and painted with glue. It was even powerful enough to have a mild gravitational effect on things in the room. Pens fell down, for example, although very slowly. Mira had the escape pods overhauled after the first convoy. After the first death. Loly. She had asked me to do it.

On the superior level, there was the bridge and the bunks, as well as a table with seats. The inferior level had no adhesive floors, so it was a 0-Gravity environment. On that level, there was a suit for space walks, an exit chamber, the engine access panels, supplies, and equipment. And also the bathroom, basically a cylinder where you want to use tubes and pipes.

\*

For a while, Mira was able to keep everything under control. She instituted routines with military precision that always had the children occupied. They would take breakfast at the same hour, and lunch and dinner. They would clean everything every day, they would have a few hours of play and Mira would read to them from the digital library, and even let them see a movie or so. And they would carefully repeat the same routine every day. Then Mira would have a couple of hours for herself while the kids slept. She would check the route towards the Mirox over and over, check the engines, check the life systems.

Only then would she go to sleep.

The kids displayed amazing discipline and restraint. She couldn't imagine any kid from Webbur with this kind of peaceful manners. They rarely gave her any trouble even though they were sad and dazed for having lost everything they owned and loved. And even though they were locked down in a small lonely ship, they didn't get bored or dismayed, they just endured. They responded very well to her, to any order whatsoever, and her routines seemed to work.

Supplies had not been meant for so many awaken people, but as most of them were children, they would last for a few weeks with little need for rationing. Every calculation told Mira they would take three weeks to reach the Mirox asteroid belt. After that, she was sure she would be able to make contact and signal for help. And three weeks... Well... They might just make it.

*

One day, though, when Mira was taking a rare shower after isolating the bathroom with the appropriate plastic sheet, she was interrupted by Hedi knocking on the cylinder.

"Captain! Captain! Please come see this!"

Mira quickly rinsed herself, got her overalls on and came out of the container.

"What is it, X.O.?"

Hedi took her to where the cryo-drawers were, one over the other. Mira looked at the monitor the girl was pointing at. There was a red light in it. An alarm. Mira checked all the numbers. There was no mistake. The child in that drawer was losing all signs of life. The vitals were decreasing steadily to neutral levels. The boy was dying.

She knew that could happen. Children in cryogenics didn't do that well. Something to do with the growing up process. It was a mess they had never quite figured out, in those days. Every time they put a child in a cryo-drawer, there was a significant chance it would go wrong.

Mira immediately looked at the vitals of all the others. Nothing particularly off.

"What do we do?" Asked Hedi.

Mira turned to her and sighed.

"There's really nothing we can do, Hedi."

The girl's eyes widened.

"What do you mean?"

Mira shook her head.

"He's dying. There's nothing we can do."

Hedi took her hand to her mouth, shocked.

"But... We could wake him up, can't we? If something is wrong with the freezing, we can take him out of it, can't we?"

Mira shook her head again.

"It doesn't work that way, darling. The harm is done. If we took him out it would only kill him faster. The cryo-liquid would grab on to his cells and tear him apart."

Hedi's eyes started to water. She contained a scream.

"You know him?" Asked Mirany.

The tears started flowing almost immediately. Mirany took her in her arms.

"Come here."

And the wailing came right after.

*

In the next few days, the rest of the cryo-drawers went into red status as well. One by one, all the vitals of the children in cryo-stasis dissolved into neutral values, dying. On the third day, Mira tried to wake one up, the one that hadn't shown any signs of trouble so far. But it was a disaster. Not only did the girl not wake up, but by the time they opened the drawer, her blood had started to spill from every single pore in her body.

The event practically destroyed the spirit of the group as well. Everyone was depressed. From the little twins to Mirany herself. She made an effort and bravely told a lot of stories and sang to the children so they would go to sleep. But she herself would cry silently to sleep every night.

For days, routines were painful, and some were forgotten altogether. Sadness seemed to dominate the small vessel. Until one day, Mirany found Jona, the 8-year-old boy, looking through the window, melancholic.

"Are you ok?"

The boy tried to smile and then confessed:

"Today is my birthday."

Mira looked at him, for a moment, and the boy showed her the date in his watch. Then she had an idea.

"That's great!" She said. "Let's do a party!"

With that pretext, she mobilized the children. They decorated the pod with anything they found, as golden sheets, flashlights and even built a kind of a fort with boxes of all kinds. They had a proper meal, as far as survival meals were concerned, and Mira even managed to make a kind of cake with some condensed milk. They sang songs and enjoyed each other's company.

That night, when Mira put them to sleep, she felt more at ease again. And that's when Hedi came to her once more.

"Captain. There's a signal!"

Mira jumped to follow her, looked at the screens and sat at the controls. There was a signal. But she quickly made the calculations. A single signal, this close to the Mirox, but on this side. On the wild side. It could be a military vessel. But it could also be miners, or scavengers, neither of which were immediately trustworthy. And it could also be pirates or, even worst, slave runners. And the *Janny* was only a few days away from the Mirox. And supplies were scarce but not that scarce. Maybe they could make it. Maybe it was better not to take the risk. She quickly operated the controls of the computer and disconnected the pod's emergency beacon.

"How long have they been out there?" She asked Hedi. "How long is the signal showing?"

"I don't know." Said the girl.

"When did you see it?"

Hedi grabbed her own shoulders, scared but not knowing why.

"Just now. I ran to tell you."

Mira looked at the screen and saw the signal approaching.

"Shit. They're very close, and they're coming here." She immediately started shutting everything down. "Get the portable heaters, Hedi. Take them next to the beds. I'm turning down the main energy. Don't wake anybody up."

She frantically changed course before shutting down the small cruise thrusters and all the lights and anything that would leave a trace to someone looking. Hedi looked at her confused, for a moment. Mira turned to her and stopped. She was so young…

"We don't know who they are, Hedi." She said. "We need to be careful."

Hedi made a little nod. Mira nodded back.

"Please go get the heaters." She asked. "I need to turn down the energy emissions."

Hedi left, and Mirany looked at the screens again. She frowned. The signal had changed course as well and was coming towards the pod. They'd spotted the engine burn. They definitely knew the pod was there. And then the signal disappeared.

"Shit…"

Mira knew what it meant. It meant the other ship had left the signal on as long as it fooled her prey, but then it had turn it off to cover her approach once it saw the pod trying to escape. It meant they were probably hostile. Mirany looked back and saw Hedi starting to turn on the heaters. She pressed the last buttons, and the energy on the pod came down to a minimum.

She looked at the blackness of Space. She couldn´t see anything out there. For now. Hedi came and stood next to her, and she held her hand.

"You think…?" Started the young girl. "You think…?"

"We don't know yet. Let's wait."

They waited for a tense few minutes, anxiously looking at the screens. And then Hedi said.

"There."

But Mira had seen her first. It wasn't a merchant. And it wasn't a combat ship. Not a frigate, a brig, or a schooner. Maybe they weren't pirates. Maybe only scavengers they'd be able to trade with. Negotiate. What were those strange things coming out of the hulls?

"What is that?" Asked the girl. Mirany quickly zoomed in. And then she gasped.

"What are those?" repeated Hedi.

Mirany was paralyzed. Her worst nightmare was coming true.

"Captain? What is that? What are those things?"

Mira swallowed hard and finally answered.

"Sacks. Those are sacks."

"Sacks? But what are they holding? What is that inside them?"

And Mirany could only whisper:

"People. Those are people. It's a slave ship."

COMING SOON


# THE DARK SEA WAR
# CHRONICLES
## Volume II


MISSION IN THE DARK

ALSO AVAILABLE
AT AMAZON

Subscribe for news and short-stories by
**Bruno Martins Soares**
at
ALEX 9 Page

# ABOUT THE AUTHOR

Bruno Martins Soares writes fiction since he was 12 years old, and his first book, 'O Massacre' (The Massacre), a collection of short-stories, came out in Portugal in 1998.

It was followed by several contributions to newspapers, magazines and other collective books.

In 1996, he won the National Young Creators Award for Writing, representing Portugal at the 1997 Torino Young Creators of Europe and the Mediterranean Fair, where his short-story 'Mindsweeper' was translated and published in Italian.

His first novel 'A Saga de Alex 9' (The Alex 9 Saga) was published in Portugal in 2012, by publisher Saída de Emergência, within a series that features authors like George R.R.Martin or Bernard Cornwell.

He worked in Project Development for Television, and was a journalist and a communications, HR and management consultant before settling as a writer. He was also an international correspondent in Portugal for Jane's Defense Weekly and a researcher for The Washington Post. He wrote several plays and short and full length pictures' screenplays, and he wrote and produced English-spoken Castaway Entertainment's full length feature film 'Regret', distributed in the USA and Canada in 2015. He lives and works in Lisbon.

Made in the USA
Monee, IL
06 May 2020